THE MANY-SPLENDORED
FISHES OF HAWAII

REVISED AND UPDATED

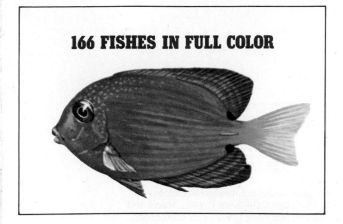

166 FISHES IN FULL COLOR

BY GAR GOODSON

•

Illustrated by Phillip J. Weisgerber
and
Edmund L. Lambert

Graphic Design and Cover by Robert Shepard

This book is dedicated to my wife, Queta. She spent many hours on Hawaiian beaches while I explored endlessly the many-splendored fishes of Hawaii. She gave unselfishly through all the trials of publication. This is her book, as well as mine.

First paperback edition published in October 1973 by Marquest Colorguide Books. Reprinted twice, the first reprinting (1977) with corrections. Reissued by Stanford University Press in 1985. For the reissue, fairly extensive revisions have been made in the text to bring scientific and common names of fishes up to date, and to correct various details of fish descriptions; four paintings have been replaced. Not published in hardcover.

Stanford University Press
Stanford, California 94305
© 1973, 1985 by Gar Goodson
Printed in Japan
ISBN 0-8047-1270-0   LC 84-40783
Last figure below indicates year of this printing:
96 95 94 93 92

PREFACE

I took my first plunge into Hawaii's underwater world off Oahu's Hanauma Bay some years ago. That dive revealed an unforgettable realm of oceanic blue, forests of coral heads, and teeming reef fishes. There were clouds of butterflies, damselfishes, and surgeonfishes rippling and gleaming in hues of yellow, blue, green, red, and black in the sea-filtered sunlight. There were long pipe-shaped fishes hanging motionless in the tides, glowing like yellow fluorescent light tubes. Great cow-like parrotfishes browsed contentedly, their peacock-colored bodies rolling and twisting as they bit chunks out of the living coral reef. I had never seen such a splendor of fishes.

After the first dive, I couldn't stay out of the water. I dove off Kona, Kauai and Maui and found strange fishes everywhere. I had to know more about them. What species were they? Why were they painted in such lavish, exquisite colors? Why did they have such odd shapes? And why did they inhabit these barren, apparently lifeless stretches of submerged lava, sand, rock and blossoming coral reefs? After years of review, research and diving off Hawaiian shores, I found answers to most (not all) of my questions. At some point during my search it occurred to me that there was a real need for a "fish-watcher's book," much like the illustrated bird-watcher books that are available in color.

This book is designed for the fish-watcher; that non-technical, curious person, whether casual tourist-swimmer, skin diver, SCUBA diver, fisherman or aquarist who seeks to know more about Hawaii's abundant and beautiful marine life. No special knowledge of fishes is required to comprehend this book, other than a general understanding of the parts of a fish. The illustration below is self-explanatory.

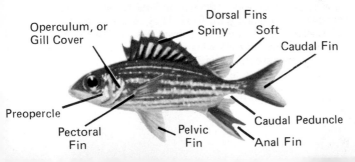

Operculum, or Gill Cover
Dorsal Fins
Spiny
Soft
Caudal Fin
Preopercle
Pectoral Fin
Pelvic Fin
Caudal Peduncle
Anal Fin

I have sought to be as accurate as possible in describing in words and pictures 170 Hawaiian fishes, out of over 600 species recorded in Hawaii, with particular focus on those commonly sighted by divers, taken by fishermen or collectors, or found in the Honolulu marketplace. Readers who desire information regarding fishes not included here, as well as keys to fish families, taxonomic details, and meristic characteristics, may refer to page 87 of this book for a bibliography of reference reading and source material.

This book is also designed to interest those who have never looked beneath the surface of the sea. The Hawaiian Islands are a fish-watcher's paradise as evidenced in these pages. All that is needed is the ability to swim and a face mask and snorkel tube. To aid the diver in locating Hawaii's coral reef fishes, and the fisherman in finding prime game-fishing areas, I have provided reef maps on pages 82-86 of this book. The guide maps locate Hawaii's splendid beaches, bays, and parks and indicate the heavier concentrations of coral reefs on the six larger islands. Also shown are preferred and proven game fishing areas, shore fishing zones, and diving areas that are well-explored and well-populated with fishes.

Oahu's Hanauma Bay, near Koko Head, is highly recommended for beginning divers and experienced aquanauts. The State of Hawaii has declared this lovely coral reef bay an underwater park, where no spear-fishing or taking of reef animals is allowed. Not surprisingly, the fishes seem to know they are safe there. They swarm into Hanauma Bay, while similar nearby reefs where spear-fishing is allowed are almost barren of fishes.

A final and important objective of this book is to remind the State of Hawaii of the magnificent and highly perishable resource that lies just off its shores. Early Hawaiians understood the sea and its resources. They depended on it heavily for food. They carefully nurtured and managed the numerous fish species, taking some for food while carefully allowing others to grow, breed, and replenish the stock. Today, the Hawaiian fisherman is virtually a memory, and industry, tourism, a great influx of people, and urban sprawl are rapidly changing the character and relation of the islands and their people with the sea. New measures of conservation and reef management are critically needed. While most of our coral reefs are still intact, some of them, such as Oahu's Kaneohe Bay, have been irreparably damaged by pollution. If the coral reefs die, whether due to despoliation by sewage, industrial wastes, or careless divers and collectors, then the reef fishes will die with them.

There is increased sensitivity today on the part of citizens, public officials, and scientists to the great need for careful management and preservation of our natural resources. The establishment of Hanauma Bay, Oahu as an underwater park was an important step in reef and fish preservation. It is hoped that this book will encourage the establishment of more underwater parks in Hawaii. Fishes of the sea, like animals of the land, need not be hunted to extinction or driven from their habitats. They are fascinating, beautiful creatures to study and admire, deserving of our care and concern. The wilderness question is especially applicable to Hawaii. Do we want to have to tell our grandchildren about the wilderness that was, and the underwater world of the reefs that used to be? Or can we preserve these frontiers, so that they can find them as we did, and experience the same joy, pleasure and admiration?

ACKNOWLEDGMENTS

This book would not have been possible without the basic groundwork laid by Jordan and Evermann in their work, "The Shore Fishes of the Hawaiian Islands," and Fowler's "The Fishes of Oceania." I am especially indebted to the very complete and painstaking Hawaiian fish handbooks produced by William A. Gosline and Vernon E. Brock ("A Handbook of Hawaiian Fishes"), and Spencer Wilkie Tinker ("A Guide to Hawaiian Fishes"). Acknowledgements to these and numerous other authors and publishers whose works were valuable in compiling this book are made in a detailed bibliography and list of reference reading on page 87 of this book.

Appreciation is also due to Ray Weil, Bill Wilson and Robert D. Kennedy, who freely offered counsel, publishing advice and encouragement when resolution faltered. Bob Kennedy made substantial, valuable improvements in language and syntax that helped make tangled fish descriptions more comprehensible. Thanks are also due to Marlys Morrison, Dave Korobkin and Robin Sitowski for service above and beyond the call of duty when the deadline was near.

Special appreciation is due to Dr. Leighton R. Taylor, Director, Waikiki Aquarium, and to Mrs. Karon Chang, Staff, Waikiki Aquarium, for the careful review and assistance they gave in the updating and correcting of the second printing of the original edition.

Special thanks are due also to Bruce A. Carlson, Curator, Waikiki Aquarium, John E. Randall, Bishop Museum, and Tyson Roberts, California Academy of Sciences, for their thorough review of all aspects of the book preparatory to publication of the Stanford reissue. Through their efforts, the book has been brought thoroughly up to date—revisions have been entered on four pages out of five, and four of the original paintings have been replaced.

CONTENTS

PART 1—THE INSHORE REEF FISHES

PART 2—THE OFFSHORE GAME FISHES AND SHORE GAME AND FOOD FISHES

FISHES OF HAWAII

PART 1

THE INSHORE REEF FISHES

BUTTERFLYFISHES

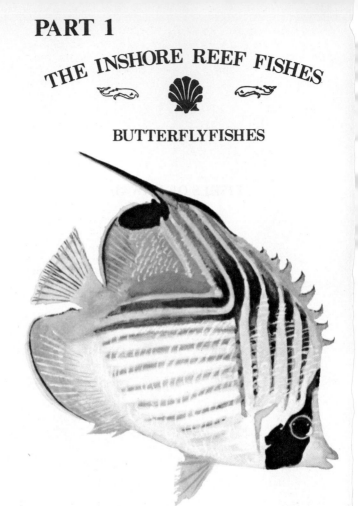

Threadfin, golden butterflyfish (lauhau) *Chaetodon auriga* This fish is distinctive for the filament or threadfin trailing from the dorsal fin. The long nose of the threadfin is well-adapted to picking coral polyps and marine organisms from crevices in the reef. Also reported to be common in the Red Sea and Australia, where it grows to 9''. For some reason, the Hawaiian threadfin reaches only about 6''.

1

Much like a marine butterfly, the butterflyfish appears in rare splendor around Hawaiian coral reefs. The islands are especially favored in having about 20 of the most delicate and brilliantly colored species, sought after by collectors of rare fish around the world. The various species display a rainbow of colors, predominating in bright yellow and pale citron, delicately spotted, striped or tinged with pale green, mauve blue, red, brown and black. Their beauty and relative scarcity make butterflyfish a breath-taking sight underwater. In numerous dives around the islands, I have seen most of the species illustrated here, singly or in pairs, occasionally in schools. Many butterfly species characteristically pair off at an early age (2" to 3" in length), and appear to remain together for life. It is not known if these are always male and female fishes, but they share the same home range in the coral reef, and will defend it fearlessly against all aggressors, especially other butterflies. The pair seem almost inseparable, and follow each other around as though attached by a string.

Four-spot or white-spot butterfly (lauhau) *Chaetodon quadrimaculatus* This is a very striking fish, with the two large white spots on each side surrounded by a grey-black area. Usually found in pairs swimming near the bottom in shallow and deeper portions of a leeward area, such as Kona. To about 6".

□ The chaetodonts are disc-shaped fishes with small mouths set with bristle-like teeth (chaeta = bristle, odont = tooth). Some, like the long-nose butterfly, have forcepslike snouts for picking small invertebrates from coral crevices. Hawaiian butterflies range in size from 4" species like the coral butterfly to the lined butterfly, which reaches over a foot in length.

□ Although they are seemingly fragile and defenseless against the numerous predators of the reef, butterflyfish are able to survive by their rapidity, agility and defensive shape and coloring. They rarely stray far from the sheltering reef, and their narrow bodies fit easily into cracks and holes in the coral. If cornered, they lower their heads and spread their dorsal and anal spines, presenting the attacker with a difficult, prickly meal to swallow. Further, as shown in the following illustrations, almost all Hawaiian butterflies possess a dark stripe or patch passing through and concealing their eyes. Many also have a false eye spot or "ocellus" located near the tail. Current theory holds that this false eye spot is designed to fool predators. The false eye spot is usually much larger than the real eye, thus confusing the attacker as

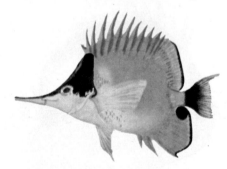

Long-nose butterfly (lau wiliwili-nukunuku-'oi'oi) *Forcipiger flavissimus* For many years it was assumed there was only one Hawaiian long-nose butterfly, the common *F. flavissimus* shown here, found everywhere off our reefs. Recent studies reveal that a close look-alike relative, *Forcipiger longirostris,* first discovered by Captain Cook off Kona in 1778, is still in residence off the Kona Coast, although very rare. While almost identical, the two fish can be identified by counting the dorsal spines—12 for *F. flavissimus,* and 10 to 11 for *F. longirostris.* Oddly, some specimens of *F. longirostris* are a solid dark black-brown in color. Both species grow to about 6".

Reticulated butterflyfish (kapuhili) *Chaetodon reticulatus* Previous reports of this fish have described it as "dusky, dark, nondescript," but in life it is actually quite beautiful, with white spots on the scale centers against a dark background, a white collar, high yellow-banded fins and a red tail-light stripe at the base of the anal fin. It is frequently sighted off the Kona Coast. To about 5".

to the size of its prey, and the location of the head of the butterfly. To add to the camouflage, butterflies may even swim backwards, making it even more difficult to tell where the head is located. Thus when the attacker lunges at the wrong end, the wily butterfly makes its escape to a nearby crevice. An occupation which the butterflies share with some angelfishes and wrasses is that of picking parasites off larger fish. This is not a fulltime occupation with butterflies, however, as it is with the Hawaiian rainbow cleaner wrasse.

Hawaiian coral, or white collar butterfly (lauhau) *Chaetodon kleinii* This rather plain butterfly is found over ledges and around coral rubble areas. It is occasionally taken in deep water, sandy bottom areas that are devoid of coral—a rare environment for butterflies, most of which are quite dependent on the coral reef. To 4".

Saddleback butterfly (kapuhili) *Chaetodon ephippium* Rare in Hawaii. After numerous dives, I am still looking forward to my first glimpse of a saddleback. They are reported to be common around Kawaihai, Hawaii. Note the filament or "threadfin" off the dorsal. Adults of both the saddleback and the threadfin butterfly possess this filament. To 6".

Pebbled butterfly (lauhau) *Chaetodon multicinctus* Small (to about 4"), delicately spotted and tinged with green and yellow, this butterfly is frequently confused with the citron or the crochet butterflies. But the distinct vertical bands serve to identify this fish.

Lined butterfly (lauhau, kikakapu) *Chaetodon lineolatus* This is the largest of the Hawaiian butterflies, attaining over a foot in length. It is a wide-ranging fish, found throughout the Indo-Pacific to Japan, and reaching South Africa. Though rare in Hawaii, it is occasionally seen on outer reefs, usually in pairs.

Lemon butterfly (lauwiliwili) *Chaetodon miliaris* This butterflyfish is a common inshore species found throughout the Hawaiian Islands and, so far, reported nowhere else. Easily identified by the crochet-like spots forming approximately 11 vertical rows from the pectoral to the anal fins. Recently divers have reported seeing this fish picking parasites off other fishes. To about 6".

Ornate, or clown butterfly (kikakapu) *Chaetodon ornatissimus* A feast for the eyes, with its gold-orange stripes and painted, clown-like face. Fairly scarce. Adults are usually seen in pairs; if you see one, the other is usually right around the corner. Prefers deeper water. To about 7".

6

Rainbow butterfly (lauhau) *Chaetodon trifasciatus* I finally sighted a pair of these splendid fish off a beach near Hana, Maui, though they are also reported frequently seen in Kaneohe Bay. They are well worth the trip, wherever sighted. Considered by many fish-fanciers to be the most beautiful of all the butterflies. The rainbow was first recorded in Sumatra in 1797. To 6".

Tear-drop butterfly kikakapu, lauhau) *Chaetodon unimaculatus* This is the outstanding Hawaiian exponent of the false eyespot or "ocellus" theory, with its large tear-drop "eye" almost in the center of its body. Since many species of butterflies seem to do nicely without the eyespot, it would seem that this bit of camouflage has outworn its usefulness (or perhaps the theory is awry). To about 6".

Bluestripe butterfly (lauhau) *Chaetodon fremblii* These lovely little fish are a welcome sight in shallow coral reef waters in Hawaii. They are numerous at Hanauma Bay and Makapuu Point, Oahu. To date, this fish has been reported only from Hawaii. It is one of the few Hawaiian butterflies that lacks a vertical bar through the eye. To 5".

Raccoon butterfly (kikakapu, kapuhili) *Chaetodon lunula* Juvenile raccoons have only a single stripe through the eye and a prominent black spot on their soft dorsal fin. By the time they reach 5", they acquire the lavish bands and stripes shown on this adult. They do have a raccoon-like appearance underwater, with the bandit-like mask over their eyes, and the smart, white collar. To about 7".

8

Pyramid butterfly (kihikihi) *Hemitaurichthys polylepis* This bright little fish is unique among Hawaiian butterflies in having large brown and yellow zones, with the curious flat-topped white pyramid at its center. It is reported to be a schooling fish, and large groups have been sighted by divers near the base of submarine cliffs. Pairs are also frequently sighted. To about 7''.

Citron butterfly (lauhau) *Chaetodon citrinellus* This fish is common in Northern Australia, very rare throughout the tropical Indo-Pacific, and for some reason has seen fit to honor Hawaii with its pale, lovely speckled-citron presence. Quite rare, even in Hawaii. The black bar along the perimeter of the anal fin is a good identifier for *C. citrinellus*. To 4''.

Tinker's butterfly (lauhau) *Chaetodon tinkeri* Once thought to be found only in Hawaii, this fish has now been discovered in the Marshall Islands and in other areas. Named after Spencer Wilkie Tinker, the Director of the Waikiki Aquarium, by Dr. Leonard P. Schultz in 1951. Grows to about 6''.

Moorish idol (kihikihi) *Zanclus cornutus* The beauty and fragility of this fish put it in a class by itself, and it is, in fact, not a butterflyfish, but belongs to the Zanclidae, a fish family of which the idol is the only member. It is actually more closely related to the surgeon fishes. Idols are usually found around Hawaiian reefs in small groups of three to six or more, probing into crevices with their long snouts for algae and small marine organisms. To about 7''.

Pennantfish, or wimplefish (kihikihi) *Heniochus diphreutes* This lovely little butterflyfish often displays cleaning behavior as a juvenile, removing parasites from larger fishes. Not uncommon off Hawaiian reefs, where it is sometimes mistaken for the Moorish idol. To about 6''.

Stripey, or convict fish *Microcanthus strigatus* Young ½'' stripeys are numerous in rocky tidepools in early spring. By May, they have grown to 2'', and feed mostly on small invertebrates. Once classed with the butterflies, the stripey was reassigned to the Scorpididae (sweep) family by Fraser-Brunner in 1945. Common in Australia and Japan. Scientists theorize that the stripey and other Japanese fishes traveled to Hawaii via such warm water currents as the Kuroshio. To 6''.

10

ANGELFISHES

Closely related to the butterflies, the angelfishes (family Pomacanthidae) are so like the butterflies that they are frequently classed in the same family. They differ from the butterflies in having a strong, sharp spine at the lower edge of each gill cover. Perhaps because of this extra weapon, which they use to good effect in battle, angelfish seem a bit more aggressive than the more timid and retiring butterflies. They are frequently seen in pairs, and like the butterflies are very sensitive about their territory. They will defend it ferociously against all comers. Angels also possess more elaborate and flowing fins than the butterflies, enabling them to maneuver rapidly and gracefully among the jagged coral heads.

Hawaiian angelfish species range in size from the dainty Fisher's angel, reaching 3", to the bandit angelfish which grows to about 7". Due to its relative isolation in the Pacific, Hawaii is not endowed with the large, colorful angelfishes found in abundance in other areas of the Pacific, such as the Philippines. Nonetheless, our angelfishes are unique in that most of them are found nowhere else in the world. Of the four angelfishes shown here, only one species, the flame angelfish, has been found outside the Hawaiian Islands.

Of the *Centropyge* genus angels, only one species, the Potter's angel, is seen with any frequency. It occurs commonly in Kaneohe Bay, Oahu and along the Kona coast. The others are only occasionally seen. Fisher's angel is fairly common at depths of 60 feet or more. Like the butterflyfishes, angels possess fine, flexible, comb-like teeth which enable them to dine on a wide variety of marine organisms, including sponges, coral, worms, algae and plankton.

Bandit angelfish *Holacanthus arcuatus* Found only in Hawaii, this black-banded angel has a natural mask, and is usually encountered at depths of 50 ft. or more. They are frequently seen in pairs. To about 7".

Potter's angelfish *Centropyge potteri* Delicately mottled in narrow ribbons of gold and mauve, this beauty is known only from Hawaii. Look for this fish in water where the bottom is composed of masses of branching coral full of crevices. To 4".

Flame angelfish *Centropyge loriculus* First discovered at Johnston Atoll, this fish has now been taken from other areas of the Indo-Pacific, including Hawaii. A beautiful and very conspicuous fish when seen in its natural habitat. To about 5".

Fisher's angelfish *Centropyge fisheri* Another rare angel, so far known only from Hawaii. 14 specimens of this small, prickly fish were dredged from 180 feet of water. It is fairly common at 60 ft. depths or more. To 3".

DAMSELFISHES

The pomacentrids, or damselfishes, are small, tropical fishes distinguishable from most other marine species in having only one nostril on each side of the snout (instead of the usual two). Hawaiian damsels are a bit drab when compared to the brilliant blue and yellow species of Florida, Bermuda and the West Indies, but they make up in personality, character and pugnacity what they lack in color. They range in size from 3" to 10", and inhabit inshore reefs and tidepools over depths from 5 to 50 feet. A few range out to 150 ft. depths. White-spotted damsels are usually found around large heads of finger coral. Hundreds of them will hover over a large head, and at the approach of a diver, instantly disappear like a shadow into coral crevices, to quickly reappear when danger is past.

☐ Two of the most common Hawaiian damsels are the *mamo* and the *kupipi*. The *mamo*, or sergeant major, is abundant in surge pools and frequently taken by shore fishermen. Gosline and Brock tell of having seen a school of some 400 *mamo* suspended like a curtain from the surface to the bottom 40 feet below. The *kupipi* and the brighteye damsel are basically surge pool forms that thrive in small reef holes, even in quite violent surge areas.

☐ Most pomacentrids spawn on the bottom, and unusual mating behavior has been reported among some species. The male fish sets up a strongly defended territory on a section of rock, and begins a series of invitations to passing females that he is ready to spawn. When an egg-bearing female sees him making his looping motions over his territory and accepts his invitation, she is led to the cleared area. Once she has deposited all her eggs, she is chased from the nest, and the male continues his looping mating signals. When several females have deposited their eggs he takes total responsibility, fanning the eggs with his fins to oxygenate them, and guarding them ferociously against all predators. Large fish and even skindivers have been chased and routed by worried male damsels. His vigil ends when the eggs hatch and the tiny damsels are left to fend for themselves on the vast, teeming reef.

Kupipi *Abudefduf sordidus* The *kupipi* is distinguished from the *mamo* by its uniform gray-brown color, and by the black spot near the tail right behind the dorsal fin. Young *kupipi* are very aggressive tide pool inhabitants, omnivorous like the *mamo*. They grow to be one of the largest of the damselfishes, to 10".

Brighteye damselfish *Plectroglyphidodon imparipennis* Distinctive for its very bright eyes, and because it is the only Hawaiian damsel of a delicate golden olive color. Often found in the more violent surge areas of rocky tide pools, where it makes its home in holes and cracks in the reef. Grows to 3".

White-spotted damsel (alo'ilo'i) *Dascyllus albisella* A glossy black fish with a pushed-in face and a bright white domino on its back. When the fish leaves cover, the white spot broadens to encompass the entire body. When near the bottom, it is greyish in color. Found only in Hawaii, where small schools form shifting black clouds over finger coral heads. To 5".

Pacific gregory *Stegastes fasciolatus* Look for this dusky little fish in quiet water on either side of the surge zone. Though one of the most numerous damsels in Hawaii, it is a solitary fish, living in coral cracks and crevices. May be distinguished from the dark-finned damsel by its bright yellow eyes. To 5".

Sergeant major (mamo) *Abudefduf abdominalis* This very hardy and aggressive fish is omnivorous, and will eat virtually anything from algae to fishermen's bait. Because of its hardiness it is a circumtropical species, and it or its close cousins are found in all shallow tropical seas. Its color is highly changeable, and it can flash from greenish, black-banded livery to a silvery or black coloration. The *mamo* is occasionally confused with the *kupipi*. To 7".

Agile damselfish *Chromis agilis* This lovely little fish is delicately tinged in olive, copper, and lavender, with a black spot at the base of the pectoral and black-edged dorsal and anal fins. Often seen in aggregations hovering over the reef. When threatened, they dive as one to shelter in the coral. To about 6".

CARDINALFISHES, AHOLEHOLE

The cardinalfishes (Apogonidae family) and the *ahole-hole* are nocturnal fishes not usually seen by the daylight diver unless he searches the darker areas of the reef. Most of the cardinals are handsomely colored in shades of red, lavender or brown, and one of the most attractive of the Hawaiian species is the spotted cardinal, shown here. Most cardinals are small fishes like the red cardinal shown which grows to about 3". Some, like the spotted cardinal, reach 6" to 8" lengths. Many cardinals are mouth brooders that take their eggs into their large mouths for incubation. They carry them in their mouths until they hatch. Hawaiians are fond of the fish as food (*upapalu* means "soft"), and they fish for them on moonlit nights, when cardinals are reported to come to the surface in large numbers, especially in Puna and Ka'u.

Red cardinalfish (upapalu) *Apogon coccineus* To 3".

Spotted cardinalfish (upapalu) *Apogon maculiferus* To 6".

☐ *Aholehole* means "sparkling," and this fish of the Kuhliidae family is a lovely, silvery sparkling animal. It grows to 12", and was considered one of the finest delicacies by early Hawaiians, both as food and as a ceremonial sacrifice. When a royal chiefess had a craving for the fat *aholehole,* runners were dispatched, and in short order the succulent fish was brought, wrapped in seaweed and still breathing, all the way from Puna to Hilo.

Silver perch (aholehole) *Kuhlia sandvicensis* To 12".

16

SURGEONFISHES, TANGS

Kole *Ctenochaetus strigosus* The bright-eyed *kole* is a lovely fish, abundant throughout Hawaii. A favorite food fish of early Hawaiians, it was frequently eaten raw and relished for its flavor. A tradition of Hawaiian housebuilding was to bury a *kole* in the ground where the easternmost houseposts would stand. This was certain insurance against bad omens. To 7″.

One of the most startling sights on my first dive into Hawaii's underwater world was a school of orangespine unicornfish. They swam by, picking and plucking at the coral, and I was so fascinated that I followed and spied on them for as long as I could hold them in view. They were so bizarre and colorful, like ancient Hawaiian underwater gods, that I felt an insatiable curiosity to know more about these fish . . . and dozens of others. So the surgeons are, in no small measure, responsible for this book.

☐ Almost all of the surgeons are beautifully colored fish, most of them are very numerous on our reefs, and they are frequently seen in schools of from 6 to 100 fish. Large schools of *manini* are almost everywhere off coral heads in Hawaii, and to see 100 or 200 of these fish rising in a silvery-green, brown-striped cloud from a coral head is a feast for the eyes. If, as sometimes occurs, you find yourself enveloped in a school of *manini*, you may discover the slightly foolish rapture that captures you as you swim along happily with the fish, wondering for a moment if maybe you weren't cut out to be a *manini.*

Hawaiian surgeon (palani) *Acanthurus dussumieri* A magnificent fish, one of the largest of the surgeons, and very abundant around Hawaii. It is also one of the most odoriferous of tangs, not recommended for eating. In Hawaiian mythology, the *palani* got its odor when it gallantly offered its back to ferry a goddess to shore. During the ride the goddess, *Ke'emalu,* lost control and urinated on the fish's back. Understandably upset, the fish god threw her in disgust back into the sea, but was never able to shake the smell. To 18".

Convict tang (manini) *Acanthurus triostegus* One of the most familiar and numerous of Hawaiian surgeons, occurring throughout the islands in small aggregations and large schools. Tiny *manini* fry lack the stripes, but begin to acquire their convict bars at about 1" in size. They grow rapidly, about ½" per month. Early Hawaiians used to net thousands of ½" *manini* spawn in early summer. Salted and dried in the sun, they were stored for later use, or taken inland for exchange with those who lived far from the shore. To 9".

Achilles tang (paku'iku'i) *Acanthurus achilles* This striking fish has colors that glow like neon underwater. Look for the *paku' iku'i* in exposed inshore reef areas where the water is turbulent. Juveniles lack the orange spot, and begin to acquire it at about 2½". To 10".

☐ The surgeonfish of the Acanthuridae family, frequently called tangs or doctorfishes, are so named for the scalpel-like spine on either side of the body just in front of the tail. The spine may more aptly be compared with a switchblade knife, since in most surgeons the blade is hinged and lies flat along the body in a sheath. When called into play, the blade flicks out and points forward, and by repeatedly sideswiping another fish, the surgeon can cause serious injury. The beginning diver need not worry about being attacked by hordes of surgeonfish. The tang, or for that matter, any fish, will rarely attack a creature larger than itself. The usual object of attack is another fish, often of the same size and species, that acts as though it may threaten the hold of the first fish on its section of reef or "territory."

Gold-rimmed surgeon, whitecheek surgeon *Acanthurus glaucopareius* A feast for the eyes, this tang is rare in Hawaii. It is closely related to the achilles tang and found in the same habitat. John Randall writes that the two fish interbreed, and have produced a hybrid tang that is intermediate in color. To 8″.

Almost all tangs have the hinged blades, but a few genera (exemplified by the *kala,* or unicorn fishes in Hawaii), have two fixed, unhinged spines on either side of the tail.

☐ Like parrotfish, tangs are herbivorous, continually searching out and cropping the reef algae. A large school of tangs may swoop down on a small coral head and leave it practically bare of algae. They are not much esteemed by fish gourmets because of the strong odor and savor of the flesh, but surgeons were highly regarded as food by early Hawaiians. The bright-eyed *kole* was a favorite food fish, as was the *manini.* Those surgeons with the most noticeable odor and taste include the *api* (sailfin tang and mustard surgeon); the *palani* (Hawaiian surgeon); the *maiko* (brown surgeon), and all of the *kala,* or unicorn fishes.

20

Whitespotted surgeon (api) *Acanthurus guttatus* Those white spots on the aft half of the fish and the yellow pelvic fins are good identifiers for this surgeon. Look for it in violent inshore surge areas, where it is frequently confused with the sailfin tang. To 12''.

Red shoulder tang, olive surgeon (na'ena'e) *Acanthurus olivaceus* The red shoulder bar is always distinctive underwater, but this fish's colors are quite changeable. The young are brilliant yellow-orange and are frequently confused with the yellow tang. At about 2'' to 2½'' they begin to acquire the red shoulder bar, and as young adults they are a soft, greenish-white with vivid orange shoulder bars. As they age, they darken to brown-olive. To 14''.

Purple or yellowfin surgeon (pualu) *Acanthurus xanthopterus* One of the largest of all the surgeons, and probably the most wide-ranging, from western Mexico to Africa. Like most of the large tangs, it is reputed to have a strong odor. Since they are herbivorous, few surgeons will take a baited hook but this pualu does and is frequently taken in Hawaii. To 20''.

21

Ringtail surgeon (pualu) *Acanthurus mata* Although sometimes confused with the purple surgeon, this pualu is nevertheless dark greenish black underwater, and shows a white-banded tail. Fairly common in Hawaii, usually found well offshore in clear water. To 18".

White-banded surgeon (maiko, maikoiko) *Acanthurus leucopareius* Large schools of *maikoiko* are frequently sighted off relatively shallow reefs, and they are a shimmering sight to see. Once thought to exist only in Hawaii, this fish has now been recorded from Marcus and Easter Islands as well. To 12".

22

Yellow tang (lau'ipala) *Zebrasoma flavescens* Yellow tangs are quite common on South Pacific coral reefs, but the Hawaiian yellow tang is distinctive for having the most brilliant chrome yellow coloration of the species. A school of *lau'ipala* is a splendid sight to see, and has been compared to the Hawaiian *ti* plant with yellow, shimmering leaves (*lau'ipala* means "yellowed *ti* leaf"). Common in Hawaii, especially in Kaelakekua Bay. To 8".

Brown surgeon (mai'i) *Acanthurus nigrofuscus* This beauty is really a lavender-brown fish with orange spots on its head and a yellow tail. Also distinguishable by the two black spots near the tail. One of the smallest surgeons of the family (*mai'i* means "tiny"), abundant in most reef areas. Rarely exceeds 7".

Sailfin tang ('api) *Zebrasoma veliferum* This striped marvel, noted for its large "sailfin" dorsal and anal fins, thrives in the wild, turbulent surge areas of the reef, as do the white-spotted surgeons, and I have frequently confused the two in the frothing water. Fish I thought were sailfins turned out to be white-spotteds when I got closer, and vice versa. The adult sailfin coloration is shown here, but the colors are quite changeable. Juveniles have black, brown and cream-striped bodies with a yellow tail, and seem to be able to switch to a solid black body with yellow stripes and tail, depending on background and lighting. A beautiful animal. To 15".

23

Bluespine unicornfish (kala) *Naso unicornis* Except for the orangespine and a few other species, all unicorn tangs have the strange horn projecting from their forehead, as shown on this fully-matured adult *kala*. It would be interesting to study this fish in its natural habitat to see what use, if any, it makes of the horn. The double lancets on each side of the tail are prominently marked in blue, almost as a warning signal. The *kala* seems to be fond of fighting, since specimens injured by caudal spines are quite common. To 24".

Orangespine unicornfish (umaumalei) *Naso lituratus* This, to my mind, is one of the most unusual and vividly beautiful fishes of Hawaii. No illustration or photograph can do it justice. It has to be seen in its natural habitat, moving through the reef sun and shadows with three or four other large unicorns, to be properly appreciated. The orange, yellow and blue markings on the black body glow like traffic lights in the marine depths. Fairly common in medium to shallow reef water, such as Hanauma Bay, Oahu. To 15".

Spotted unicornfish (kala) *Naso brevirostris* When this fish reaches 12" to 18", it does have a very long horn, similar to *Naso unicornis*, above. The 6" juvenile shown here is just beginning to acquire its horn. Note that the axis of the horn in this fish is about in the center of the eye, while in *Naso unicornis* (above), the axis is above the eye. This is a good way to distinguish between these two very similar species. To 18".

24

WRASSES

In spite of being the gaudiest and most abundant family of fishes in Hawaii, the labridae, or wrasses, are not particularly noticeable to the casual diver. They are carnivorous fishes, living for the most part a solitary, predatory existence. They stay close to reef or bottom cover, and at the approach of a diver they vanish into the coral, or plummet like a shot to bury themselves in the sand. Many wrasses have the curious habit of burying themselves in the sand at night, and aquarium watchers are frequently surprised to find that a tank filled with wrasses by day will be completely barren at night—they are all tucked away sleeping in the bottom sand or gravel. Closely related to the parrotfishes, the wrasses have many characteristics in common with the parrots. The little Hawaiian rainbow cleaner wrasse likes to spin himself a gelatinous cocoon "nightgown" for protection while sleeping at night, as do many parrotfish.

☐ The colors of many of the labrids are astonishing in their beauty and variety. They glisten with gem-like spots, flecks, diamonds, blotches, club and worm-like stripes, saddles, reticulations and bars. Like the parrots, the wrasses almost defy classification due to the startling color changes that occur as the fish mature. To add to the confusion, profound color changes occur when females change into male wrasses.

☐ Certain young juvenile wrasses become sexually mature as small as 1½ inches, and mate in groups. Group mating usually begins with upward spawning rushes by an egg-laden female. She is followed by numerous young males, all of whom assist in fertilizing eggs. A certain number of the males, and apparently some sex-reversed females, become terminal-phase supermales, emerging in brilliant hues of blue, green, red or yellow, and sporting flowing, lyre-like tails. These supermales tend to mate and spawn individually with one or more females. Dominant supermale wrasses of some species set up "harems" on the reef of from 4 to 10 females and actively mate with all members of the harem. If the supermale dies or is dispatched by a predator, the largest female in the

JUVENILE

ADULT

Red labrid, yellow-tail wrasse (lolo, hinalea aki lolo) *Coris gaimard*
The *lolo*, or "lazy fish" as it is known to Hawaiians, is a brilliant
example of the color changes that occur as a typical wrasse matures. For many years the small red labrid with the white diamonds
pictured was known as *"Coris greenovii"*, while the familiar yellow-
tail wrasse or *lolo* shown was known as *Coris gaimard*—two separate species. The breakthrough came when someone discovered a
"Coris greenovii" slowly turning into a *Coris gaimard.* The trans-
formation begins when the fish is about 1½" in length. By the
time the fish is 2 to 2½" long, the metamorphosis is complete.
The adult is called *lolo* or "lazy fish" because it spends a good
deal of its time buried in the sand with only its nose protruding.
The adult yellow-tail wrasse grows to about 15".

harem changes into a supermale, and assumes the domi-
nance and mating duties of the harem. On the larger
reefs, some wrasse species have a mating system whereby
several dozen large supermales set up spawning territories
in a restricted area of the reef. Each guards his area
strongly against younger male wrasses. Each day near
midday, females come to this area and select the largest
and most brightly-colored supermale for mating. Large
supermales often spawn more than 40 times a day, and
in high population areas, 100 times a day is not unusual.
Small wonder that wrasses are so numerous.

□ In size, labrids vary from small species that attain a
maximum length of 2" up to huge bull males of other
species that reach several feet in length. Although their
flesh is soft and pasty, unattractive as food, early Hawaiians often ate certain wrasses (*hinalea* types), considering

26

them after-dinner delicacies. *Hinalea* fish were also offered to the gods as sacrifices to bring on pregnancy and to cure mental illness. The strange little bird wrasse with its long bird-like beak is known to Hawaiians as *hinalea-'aki lolo*, or "the brain-nibbler fish." It was their belief that, when eaten by the patient, the fish would go straight to the afflicted brain, nibble away the bad parts and restore the patient to a sound mind.

☐ One of the great breakthroughs in the study of fish behavior occurred when researchers discovered the mutual "gentlefish's agreement" that exists between certain species of cleaner fishes and the larger fishes they clean of parasites. In Hawaii, the brilliant little rainbow wrasses turn their home base coral heads into cleaning stations, and larger fish come and often wait in line to be cleaned. It is an incredible sight to see these tiny fish fluttering about the fins, gills, and even into the mouths of huge groupers and moray eels, predators that could easily dispatch them in a single gulp.

Rainbow wrasse, cleaner wrasse (hinalea) *Labroides phthirophagus*
These are the famous little beauties that set up cleaning stations throughout our reefs. Their single duty in life seems to be that of keeping larger fishes clean of parasites, at the same time, of course, being assured of all the parasites they can eat. When several of these wrasses were introduced to a large tank at the New York Aquarium, the directors were a little worried. The other inhabitants of the tank were large groupers and moray eels from the Atlantic, and they could never have seen a Hawaiian cleaner wrasse before. Nevertheless, the aquarium reports, "within 5 minutes all the groupers were lying on the bottom of the tank, mouths wide open, gill covers extended, while the tiny cleaner wrasses swam over and under, in the gills and out the mouth." To 5".

27

Black-banded wrasse (hilu) *Coris flavovittata* A very plentiful wrasse, popular as food with the early Hawaiians. Hawaiian legend tells of how a god, *Ma'i'o* appeared one day off Oahu swimming in the guise of a fish. Not knowing he was a god, the fishermen caught him, cut him up and distributed his flesh to the people. This so angered the gods that they brought floods down on

the hapless Hawaiians, killing all except those who worshipped the *hilu* fish. This brought *Ma'i'o* back to life in the form of the black-banded wrasse. The stripes show where his body had been touched with fire, or slashed for salting. Adult males of this species are bluish-green in color and grow to 2 feet in length. Males were formerly thought to be a separate species, *C. lepoma*, until researchers, puzzled by the absence of young specimens on the reefs, finally discovered that *C. lepoma* was really the adult male phase of the *hilu* fish. To 24''.

Saddle wrasse (hinalea lauwili, a'ala'ihi) *Thalassoma duperrey* Known only from Hawaii and one of our most numerous wrasses, the saddle wrasse is found in the rocky areas of Waikiki and in reef areas like Kaneohe Bay. This fish matures through various color changes before it attains the adult coloration shown here. Juveniles have no brown saddle, and sport a prominent stripe from eye to tail. To 12''.

Eight-lined wrasse *Pseudocheilinus octotaenia* This multi-striped little fish is usually found in coral rubble areas, and is quite shy and retiring. It takes a very stealthy diver to even glimpse this fish before it takes cover in the rubble. To 6''.

Four-lined wrasse *Pseudocheilinus tetrataenia* This little beauty has a vivid tinge to its body reminiscent of the rainbow cleaner wrasse. A joy to see on the reef, but like the 8-lined wrasse, very shy and difficult to catch out of its nest. To 4".

Sunset wrasse (hinalea) *Thalassoma lutescens* A truly striking fish with its blue-green body, orange-red head, and the curved lines radiating from the eye. Not common in Hawaii, this fish is also found in Mexican waters and is quite common from La Paz to Cabo San Lucas. Found near rocky substrates feeding on algae, crustaceans, and coral. To 7".

Scarlet wrasse *Pseudocheilinus evanidus* Like its 4-lined and 8-lined wrasse cousins, the scarlet wrasse lives a solitary existence on the reef bottom. Its prime food source is small invertebrates which roam the reef bottom adjacent to the coral heads. To 4".

Snowflake wrasse ('opule, hilu) *Anampses cuvier* This red-green tinged beauty has to be seen on the reef to be appreciated. The white-tipped scales gleam in the depths like snowflakes on a moonlit night. 2" juveniles (not shown) are plain light green with a prominent round black spot at the base of the last dorsal and anal rays. At 2½" they begin to acquire the white spots. At 3" they are mature. To 15".

Long-finned razorfish (laenihi) *Xyrichthys pavo* This fish's Hawaiian name *laenihi* means "narrow forehead," and refers to the very compressed, razor-like head most razor fishes possess, shaped almost like the prow of a ship. Since they spend much of their time burrowing into the gritty reef sand and gravel, a narrow forehead is a distinct asset. The flag-like first dorsal spine and 3 cross bars are good identifiers. To 15".

Hawaiian hogfish ('a'awa) *Bodianus bilunulatus* A popular food fish, and one of the most common labrids in the Honolulu market. Shown is the juvenile hogfish wearing its most billiant coloration. As the fish matures, the colors fade to browns and black. Frequently taken by hook and line at over 100 foot depths. To 24".

Pearlscale razorfish *Novaculichthys taeniourus* If you are diving over a sandy patch of the reef and you see a large-headed fish dive straight for the sand and disappear, that will be a razorfish. They are specialists at burying themselves in the sand when danger threatens. This labrid is distinctive for its pearly scales and four stripes radiating from the eye. To 10".

Old lady wrasse (hinalea luahine) *Thalassoma ballieui* Found only in Hawaii, the old lady wrasse is one of the largest members of the genus, reaching lengths up to 2 feet. It gets the name "old lady" due to its greyish mottled color which seems to darken with age. Older fishes are almost black, but retain the checkerboard body pattern.

Ornate wrasse (la'o, 'ohua, pa'awela) *Halichoeres ornatissimus*
A truly beautiful animal that undergoes various color changes before attaining this adult coloration. The small black mark behind the eye is always visible, however, to aid identification. One source states that early Hawaiian fishermen could tell how things were going at home by the actions of this wrasse. If a bad-tempered fisherman saw the *pa'awela* cutting capers in the water while he was fishing, he went home to beat his wife! To 8".

Red-tail wrasse *Anampses chrysocephalus* This fish was discovered by Dr. John Randall, a leading authority and photographer of Indo-Pacific fish. Shown is the female and immature male coloration. The adult male is a lavishly-decorated animal known as the "psyche-head" due to the pattern of brilliant orange lines on its head. So far known only from Hawaii. To 4".

Red shoulder wrasse, belted wrasse ('omaka) *Stethojulis balteata* This is the female of the species, and while not as gaudy as the electric green, peacock-like male, she has a delicate beauty all her own. Some females experience a sex-reversal, to emerge as brilliant, green-striped supermales. Both male and female retain the red shoulder patch at the pectoral fin base. To 5".

Malamalama (hilu) *Coris ballieui* Malamalama means "light colored" and the females of this species are quite light colored in hues of pink, yellow, and white, whereas males are striped and striated with blue lines and grow larger. Named after M. Ballieu, who was a French consul in Hawaii around 1875. To 14".

Bird wrasse, longface, beakfish (hinalea 'i'iwi, hinalea aki lolo) *Gomphosus varius* All wrasses swim with a queer hopping motion, since they use only their wing-like pectoral fins for slow cruising about the reef. This hopping motion combined with the long beak makes the bird wrasse appear especially bird-like. The illustration shows a mature male. The lower illustration is the rose-tinged female of the species. Until quite recently, these fish were considered two different species. *Hinalea 'i'iwi* means "like the *iwi* bird." Quite common off our reefs. To 10".

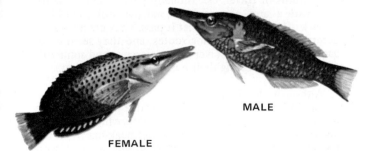

MALE

FEMALE

32

PARROTFISHES, UHU

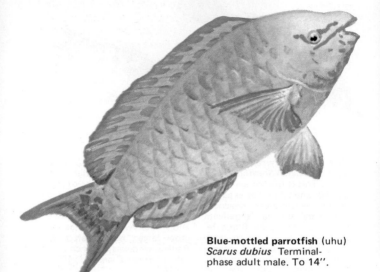

Blue-mottled parrotfish (uhu)
Scarus dubius Terminal-
phase adult male. To 14".

If you dive off Oahu's Hanauma Bay as the tide is coming in, you will encounter dozens of huge, gaudy parrotfish, or *uhu*. They swarm in over the reef in blue-green,
grey and rust-colored waves, grazing like guernsey cows
through the coral. Parrots are such large fish that they
must wait for high tide to flood the close-packed coral reefs
to give them room to maneuver and feed. They are
single-minded gentle creatures of habit, and they have their
set patterns of travel. Occasionally I have come nose-to-
nose with a large parrotfish in a narrow defile, and I had
to back off respectfully and let it pass. They are not easily
deterred from their feeding routes, and they seem to re-
gard the curious skin diver with tolerance and some irri-
tation for interrupting their non-stop, movable feast.

☐ Although closely related to the carnivorous wrasses,
parrotfish are herbivores of the Scaridae family. They are
named for their parrot-like beaks with which they bite
away chunks of coral, leaving distinct beak-marks on the
reef. In their constant quest for food, they are highly ef-
ficient recycling mechanisms. As they graze algae off the

reefs, they turn coral and rock into fine sand. They extract the algae by crushing the rock-hard coral with powerful plate-like pharyngeal teeth located in the back of the throat, then pass this stony rubble down their apparently cast-iron digestive tract. Due to their set patterns of travel, and their almost constant defecation, they leave mounds and floors of fine sand and undigested coral rubble throughout the reef.

☐ Recent interest and knowledge of the scarids, speeded by the advent of scuba diving, has revealed that parrotfish undergo dramatic color changes as they mature and, like the wrasses, sex changes as well. Many species mature through three different color phases, including juvenile, adult and "terminal phase" colorations. Male and female adults often share the same color pattern, but some males, as well as certain sex-reversed females, will mature into terminal phase "super males," sporting gaudy peacock colors and hues. The reasons for these changes and the processes by which they occur are not understood, but they are a subject of intense study in ichthyological circles. This startling new information has brought chaos to the inexact science of giving scientific names to the parrots. Of some 350 previous species of parrotfishes recorded throughout the world, a recent study reduced this number to 80 species, and many of these are in doubt. On-going studies continue to demonstrate that various fishes previously considered to be different species were actually male and female, or juvenile and adult specimens of the same fish.

**Red-lipped
parrotfish** (uhu)
Scarus rubroviolaceous
Terminal-phase adult male. To 20".

Banded-nose parrotfish (uhu)
Scarus perspicillatus Terminal-
phase adult male. To 2 ft.

Banded-nose parrotfish (uhu)
Scarus perspicillatus
Adult female. To 2 ft.

☐ Shown here are some of the more common Hawaiian parrotfish species that have been sighted and taken regularly off our reefs. Some of them, like the red-lipped parrotfish and the star-eye parrotfish, have been correlated with identical or very similar South African species. Others, like the banded-nose parrot and the blue-mottled parrot, seem to be endemic to Hawaii. In spite of fairly recent studies on the subject, the classification of Hawaiian parrotfish species is still in a chaotic state. The scientific names given to the parrots illustrated here are, at best, guesses arrived at from a welter of conflicting material. It is my hope that a thorough review and re-classification of all Hawaiian scarids will soon be initiated. They are highly visible, fascinating and beautiful fishes, easy to locate and study. Their complex life cycle and life style are still shrouded in mystery, and deserve investigation.

☐ To illustrate the startling difference between the male and female parrotfishes, I have included a terminal-phase male of the banded-nose parrot species, along with a typical rust-colored female. This distinct color differentiation

35

between the sexes is typical of all the parrots. The females of the blue-mottled parrot, for example, are dull brown to black in color, as are immature and young males of this species. In general, it is safe to say that most of the green, blue, and lavishly striped and mottled parrotfishes are adult terminal-phase males, while most of the dull grey, red or brownish-colored parrots are females or immature males. To make matters even more confusing, tiny juvenile parrots 2" to 4" long of almost all Hawaiian species are colored a light grass green, with various stripes, bars and other markings across the body that differ, depending on the species.

☐ Parrotfishes vary greatly in size. Most Hawaiian species range from 1 to 2 feet in length. There have been reports of some Indo-Pacific parrots attaining lengths of 6 feet, and scattered claims of massive old bull males reaching 12 feet in length and 6 feet in depth. Even more strange, Jacques Yves Cousteau tells of seeing huge bumphead parrotfish of the *Bolbometapon muricatus* species charging at high speeds and smashing their curious, bumper-like heads into the reef to dislodge pieces of coral, which they would then munch contentedly in the manner of most parrots. Another remarkable characteristic of certain parrots and a few wrasses is their habit of fabricating a mucous cocoon or "sleeping bag" around themselves before bedding down in the coral at night. How and why the cocoon is made is a mystery. One theory postulates that the mucous cocoon serves to protect the sleeping fish from such night predators as moray eels, which depend on their keen sense of smell to locate their prey.

Stareye parrotfish (uhu) *Calotomus carolinus* Terminal-phase adult male. To 18".

GOATFISHES

Whitespot goatfish (kumu) *Parupeneus porphyreus* One of the commonest inshore species and a favorite of spearfishermen. The *kumu* is a sociable fish, and small groups of them are often seen mingling freely with tangs, wrasses and damselfish. To 16".

The abundant and colorful goatfishes are among the most prized fishes in Hawaii for food, and include the *moano, weke, malu* and *kumu.* The goatfish played an important part in early Hawaiian sacrificial ceremony. While the pig was one of the most important offerings to the gods, it was also very precious and frequently not available. Hawaiians felt that each creature of the land had its counterpart in the sea, and goatfish were considered to be "sea pigs." If a pig could not be found for sacrifice, a goatfish would do as well. Red and white species of goats were frequently used as offerings to launch canoes, insure pregnancy, dedicate oneself to the hula school, or atone for a sin. The eating of certain goatfish at certain times of the year is said to cause "nightmare," or a kind of delirium which paralyzes the mind temporarily. Thirty to forty Japanese laborers ate goatfish on one occasion on Molokai and were "mentally paralyzed" for hours afterward. The sensation is reported to be "one of having lost balance, and feeling that the head is lower than the feet." All cases soon recovered.

Black-spotted goatfish (malu) *Parupeneus pluerostigma* This is one of the non-schooling varieties, usually found singly around coral heads at 10 or 25-foot depths. Frequently caught with hook and line, using shellfish bait. An excellent food fish. To 16".

Red or yellowstripe goatfish (weke) *Mulloides vanicolensis* A large school of these brilliant pink and yellow-striped fish is a splendid sight to see. They often school in large circular patterns. One school off Waianae was seen within 20 feet of the same place at 6-month intervals. To 16".

38

□ A distinctive characteristic of the goats is their long tactile and highly-sensitive barbels under the chin, with which they work constantly and busily about the reef bottom, probing for small crustaceans and worms. Some species are solitary, while others gather in schools, especially as adults. Some goats are noted for their ability to change color to match their background, probably as a protective device. Goatfishes are members of the Mullidae family, and they are surmullets, not to be confused with the true mullets, which belong to the Mugilidae family.

White goatfish (weke, weke'a'a) *Mulloides flavolineatus* This is the white variety frequently used in Hawaiian ceremonies calling for the sacrifice of a white weke. A popular dish, it is also suspected of producing hallucinations, weird nightmares, and depression, especially when eaten in the months of June, July and August. To 18".

Black-banded goatfish (moano) *Parupeneus multifasciatus* A common market fish. Goatfish colors are quite changeable, and they can easily shift coloration to blend with their background. This fish is quite variable, and tends to lighten its colors in daylight, and darken them in shadow or at night, as do most goats. To 12".

39

SQUIRRELFISHES

The Hawaiian holocentrids, commonly known as squirrel-fishes or soldierfishes, include the 'ala'ihi and the *men-pachi* or *'u'u*. They are primarily nocturnal fishes, with large, squirrel-like eyes and red coloration. During the day most of the squirrels hide in their crevices, and are rarely seen. They become active at night, when their dark red hues make them almost invisible, and their keen eyes enable them to forage across the dark reef for shrimps, crabs and other crustaceans. They are very rough, spiny, prickly fishes, not attractive meals to bigger fishes, and the 'ala'ihi squirrels (*Sargocentron, Neoniphon* genera) possess a sharp spine at the base of the gill cover with which they can inflict painful, sometimes poisonous wounds. The 'ala'ihi are not much used as food owing to their small size and spiny bodies. The *menpachi* and *'u'u* (genus *Myr-pristis*), however, are excellent food fish and command a high price in the Honolulu market. The squirrelfishes have recently been reclassified, and some groups that were previously ranked as subgenera have been given full generic rank, on the basis of an exhaustive study of the holocentrids.

Longjawed squirrelfish *Sargo-centron spiniferum* One of the largest of the squirrels, reaching lengths up to 2 feet. Also noteworthy for the single large spine jutting back from its long jaws, with which it can inflict painful wounds.

Deepwater squirrelfish *Pristi-lepis oligolepis* A very distinctive squirrel with large scales tipped with striking white spots. Not seen by many divers, because it dwells in much deeper water than most other squirrelfish. Grows to over 12".

Bikini squirrelfish ('ala'ihi) *Sargocentron microstoma* The coloration of the squirrelfish is variable, depending on the available light in the caves and holes which they frequent. The color of this little beauty can change from brick-red stripes to orange stripes. The stripe along the top edge of the dorsal is distinctive. To 7".

Hawaiian striped squirrelfish ('ala'ihi) *Sargocentron xantherythrum*. This fish became famous when strange noises emanated from a tank of Hawaiian striped squirrels at the Steinhart Aquarium in San Francisco. Nearby scientists and TV technicians were puzzled by the sounds, and closer scrutiny revealed the noises were coming from a pair of amorous squirrels that were holding their tails together, their bodies in the form of a V. This strange behavior was thought to be courting activity. One of the most abundant squirrels of Hawaii's outer reefs. To 7".

Pink squirrelfish ('ala'ihi) *Sargocentron punctatissimum* Like the Bikini squirrel, this fish also has a brilliant red band along the top edge of its dorsal fin, which it raises like a plume when threatened. However, the pink squirrel lacks the horizontal body stripes of the Bikini, and can easily be distinguished by its silvery pink and white body. To 6".

Bigeye squirrelfish ('u'u, menpachi) *Myripristis amaenus* The bigeye squirrelfish are the most sought-after fish in Hawaii, for they lack the prickly bodies of the other squirrels, grow much larger (to 14"), and make excellent eating. Like many other squirrels, bigeyes often aggregate in caves during the day. Shown here is the common Hawaiian bigeye. This and another close look-alike relative, *Myripristis murdjan* (not shown), grow to 14". *M. chryseres* and *M. kuntee* (not shown), also close look-alikes to *M. amaenus,* reach only about 8" to 10".

Brown-spotted squirrelfish ('ala' ihi) *Neoniphon sammara* This squirrel is easily identified by its brownish spots and stripes, in contrast to all other Hawaiian squirrels which have red stripes and markings. Also distinctive for the check-like mark on the dorsal fin. Quite common in deeper water. To 12".

Prickly or wistful squirrelfish *Plectrypops lima* Due to their large eyes and down-curving jaws, all squirrels seem to wear a wistful expression. All of them (with the exception of the *menpachi*) are also very prickly fish, rough to the touch because of their comb-like, rough-edged scales. This little brute is one of the more wistful and prickly of a wistful, prickly family. Not uncommon in Hawaii. To 7".

Aweoweo or bigeye *Priacanthus cruentatus* This "bigeye" is not a squirrelfish, although it is sometimes confused for one because of its reddish color, large eyes and nocturnal feeding activity. The *'aweoweo* is a member of the Priacanthidae family, and may be easily distinguished from the squirrels by its continuous dorsal fin. A good food fish and a favorite of spear fishermen. Variable in color, ranging from a mottled brickish red to silvery. To 12".

Diadem or crown squirrelfish ('ala'ihi) *Sargocentron diadema* One of the most brilliantly red fishes of the sea, especially when seen in its natural reef setting. Truly a diadem among squirrelfishes, distinctive also for its black-striped dorsal, which is raised and lowered frequently like a banner. To 6".

HAWKFISHES, MORWONGS

Hawkfishes (*pili koa*) of the Cirrhitidae family get their avian name from their habit of perching in the branches of coral heads or in rocky crevices, and swooping rapidly on smaller fishes and crustaceans. Hawkfishes will sit for hours in motionless vigil, punctuated by sudden dashes for food. In this and other features, hawks bear close resem-

Arc-eyed hawkfish (pili koa)
Paracirrhites arcatus To 4".

Freckled hawkfish (pili koa)
Paracirrhites forsteri To 9".

43

Magpie morwong
Cheilodactylus vittatus
To 12".

blance to the scorpionfishes. Like the scorpions, hawks possess enlarged, thickened pectoral fins which support them on their rocky perches. The arc-eyed hawkfish shown is distinctive for the bright orange circle extending up and back from the eye. It is one of the few coral fishes known that seems to advertise its vulnerable eye, rather than concealing it as do most reef fishes. The freckled hawkfish has the rather odd color pattern of speckles on the head with a horizontally striped posterior—a combination found in no other coral fish. A most unusual fish is the magpie morwong. One of these bizarre creatures was on display at the Waikiki Aquarium on my last visit there, and it is an odd sight indeed. Although its habits and lifestyle are quite similar to the hawkfish, the morwong is actually a member of the Cheilodactylidae family. The morwong is found occasionally in the Honolulu market, and is reputed to be an excellent food fish. It is also a common fish off Australian reefs, where it got the name morwong.

SCORPIONFISHES

Hawaiian turkeyfish, scorpionfish (nohu pinao) *Pterois sphex*
A venomous little fish gaining great popularity with marine aquarists. The discovery by professional fish importers that certain scorpions when mated are capable of producing as many as 6,000 fry at one spawning has flooded the marine aquarium market with tiny, attractive turkeyfish. Common on Hawaiian reefs. To 10".

This bizarre, dangerous, yet fascinating family of fishes has been given many names, including scorpionfish, turkeyfish, zebrafish, dragonfish, tiger- and lionfish, cardinal scorpionfish, rockfish, cobrafish and many others. It is a family to which most of these names do apply, due to its fearless and aggressive nature and the odd appearance and lifestyle of its members. The Hawaiian turkeyfish combines a luxuriantly spiny, almost feathery-appearing body with poisonous spines and flap-like appendages dangling from its cheeks. Many of the scorpionfishes are extremely poisonous, and should never be handled without a net or some other protective device. Such names as "scorpion" and "cobrafish" come from the venomous potential of the dorsal, anal and ventral fin spines, which can give the careless fisherman or diver a very painful puncture wound. The scorpions have never been known to kill humans, although several cases were almost fatal. The Indo-Pacific stonefishes possess a venom so powerful that an agonizing death can occur shortly after a puncture. Fortunately, there are no stonefishes in Hawaii.

☐ The scorpaenid fishes are also noteworthy because of the bony plates under their eyes, and they include several hundred species. They occur at all depths in Hawaii from a few feet of water to over one half mile, but are most prevalent at depths of about 500 feet. Their almost nightmarish appearance and improbable appendages would seem to be the antithesis of what a streamlined fish configuration should be, but as with all things in nature, the scorpionfish is well-designed for its job. It is a master at camouflage, and it waits quietly and patiently in an algae-covered crevice, frequently hanging upside down, where it looks almost exactly like part of the reef. When a small fish or crustacean comes to examine the algae-like appendages which dangle from its face, the scorpion engulfs the curious intruder with surprising rapidity. They do make fascinating pets for aquarium owners, but let the buyer beware when buying scorpionfish. One report tells of an aquarist who inadvertently grabbed and was punctured by a scorpionfish. He immediately felt shooting pains in his arm, and eventually fell to his knees. After a tourniquet was applied he was rushed to a nearby hospital, where injections put him on the road to a speedy recovery.

Hawaiian lionfish (nohu) *Dendrochirus barberi.* This scorpionfish is just as venomous as *Pterois sphex,* but due to its comparatively drab appearance and short spines, it is not as likely to attract attention. Like *Pterois sphex,* it is quite fearless, perhaps because it knows it has a very potent weapon. To 7".

Short-spined scorpionfish (nohu) *Scorpaenodes parvipinnis* An unassuming and plain little scorpion which is quite abundant in shallow water in Hawaii. It perches patiently on reef rocks and ledges, waiting for a passing meal. Because of its immobility and perfect camouflage, it is overlooked by most divers. To 6".

TRIGGERFISHES, HUMUHUMU

Painted triggerfish (humu humu nuku nuku apua'a) *Rhinecanthus aculeatus* Sometimes called the "Picasso fish," this trigger is beautifully scribed and striped. *Humu humu* means "to fit pieces together" in Hawaiian, perhaps referring to its nest-building habit. *Nuku nuku apua'a* means "nose like a pig." Note the rows of black spines near the tail, used for sideswiping and slapping enemies. To 9".

A cursory look at the triggerfish of the Balistidae family convinces many people that it is an ugly, badly designed, brainless-looking fish of little value. Even the early Hawaiians held the trigger in low esteem as food, frequently using dried triggers as "firewood" to cook other, more savory fish. But closer examination shows it to be a fascinating, attractive animal with a perky disposition and a peculiar "hide and lock" defense mechanism. Probably because they are such slow swimmers, triggers have developed a number of protective devices. When attacked or frightened, the trigger dives straight for its hole or nest in the coral and erects its large first dorsal fin, which is locked in place by the second sliding dorsal spine or "trigger."

Thus wedged into its hole, there is no way a predator fish can remove the trigger and it is usually left alone.

☐ Although seemingly grotesquely configured, with their eyes almost in the center of their bodies, the carnivorous triggers are perfectly designed to prey upon prickly crustaceans, mollusks and echinoderms. Triggers are one of the few animals that can attack a spiny sea urchin with impunity. Since their eyes are so far back in their heads, safe from the spines, they can bite the urchin's spines off with their sharp teeth, throw the urchin on its back, and

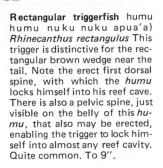

Rectangular triggerfish humu humu nuku nuku apua'a) *Rhinecanthus rectangulus* This trigger is distinctive for the rectangular brown wedge near the tail. Note the erect first dorsal spine, with which the *humu* locks himself into his reef cave. There is also a pelvic spine, just visible on the belly of this *humu*, that also may be erected, enabling the trigger to lock himself into almost any reef cavity. Quite common. To 9".

feast on the soft underbelly. Another technique learned by the intelligent trigger to obtain food is the art of using water as a tool. The triggerfish has been seen to blow jets of water at the base of a strolling sea urchin, until it is finally bowled over by the force of the jets. Once on its side, the urchin becomes a meal for the hungry trigger. The bodies of triggers are covered with hard, plate-like scales, forming a flexible yet solid armor. The tails of some species are equipped with rows of spines, and they are adept at side-swiping and tail-whipping an enemy.

☐ Very noticeable in balistids is their ability to rotate the eyes independently, enabling them to observe two different scenes at once. They swim by undulating the soft dorsal and anal fins languidly, bringing their tail into action only when speed is required.

Pinktail triggerfish (humu humu hi'ukole) *Melichthys vidua* When seen on the reef this glossy green-black fish with its pink tail and gossamer fins rimmed in black is very striking. The pinktail is known, as are most triggers, for the grunting sound it makes when taken out of the water. The grunts are produced by vibrations of the swim bladder. *Humu humu hi' ukole* means "*humu* with the pink tail." Fairly common. To 10".

Whiteline triggerfish (humu humu umaumalei) *Sufflamen bursa* A soft, delicately colored beauty, distinctive for its white accent marks and the dark, scimitar-shaped bars running down its cheek to the pectoral base. In some whitelines, these bars are golden-yellow, and are the source of the Hawaiian name, *humu humu umaumalei*, or "the *humu* wearing the lei." Though some triggers in other parts of the Pacific are reported to be violently poisonous, Hawaiian triggers appear to be safe to eat. Some however are reported to cause a "puckery" feeling in the throat—one of the first symptoms of having eaten a poisonous fish. To 8".

Crosshatch triggerfish, sargassum triggerfish *Xanthichthys mento* Thanks to its crosshatch coloration, this trigger illustrates the plate-like armor scales possessed by most triggers. The adult crosshatch likes fairly deep water, and is usually found at depths of 50 feet or more. These fish have been seen on occasion in large schools hovering 20 or 30 feet off the bottom. To 12".

FILEFISHES

Brown filefish ('o'ili lepa) *Cantherhines sandwichensis* One of the commonest filefish in Hawaii. The Hawaiian name means "flag-bearing *'o'ili*," and this fish does carry its first dorsal spine high and proud like a banner. To 7".

The filefishes of the family Monacanthidae are very closely related to the triggerfishes. Like the triggers they possess trigger-like dorsal spines which they use in the same hide-and-lock manner. Filefishes are distinguished by the fact that their first dorsal spine is located well forward, usually over the eye, while on the triggerfish the first dorsal spine is placed well in back of the eye. Filefish also have much narrower bodies than the triggers and possess a skin that is almost file-like (hence the name), compared to the plate-like scales of the triggers. The Hawaiian name for some of the filefishes is *'o'ili*, which means "make a sudden appearance." The name seems to stem from the fact that certain filefishes, and particularly the fan-tailed filefish, have the strange habit of "making sudden appearances" in great numbers from time to time over the years. The early Hawaiians believed that the appearance of the fishes prophesied the death of a great king or chief. In the spring of 1944, millions of dead fantail filefish were washed up on the beaches of southeastern Oahu. They continued coming in for weeks and created a public nuisance. More recently, thousands of fantails were seen floating dead on the ocean surface off Kauai. Strangely, in other years the fish are almost absent. Scientists surmise that cold ocean currents were responsible for the mass deaths.

White filefish (loulu) *Aluterus monoceros* The *Aluterus* genus filefish grow quite large, and this fish is no exception. The Hawaiians named the *loulu* after an indigenous palm tree which is greenish white in color. One report states that in early Hawaiian ceremony, this fish was used to cause death by the *kahuna,* or priest. To 17".

Scribbled trigger, longtail filefish (loulu) *Aluterus scriptus* These are not recommended for small aquariums since, while they start out small and attractive, they grow to over 2 feet in length. Famed for its broomlike tail and its powder-blue scribbles, this fish is widespread in tropical seas, and is found as far as the Caribbean.

Brown-spotted filefish ('o'ili) *Cantherhines verecundus* (previously designated *Amanses pardalis*) A very small and fairly common filefish that is popular with aquarists because it won't outgrow the tank. Filefish are much less aggressive than are the triggerfish, partially because their mouths are considerably smaller, and so are their appetites. To about 5".

Fan-tailed filefish ('o'ili 'uwi 'uwi) *Pervagor spilosoma* The Hawaiian name means "squealing *'o'ili,*" and refers to the grunting or squealing noises that both filefish and triggerfish make when they are taken from the water, produced by vibrations of the fish's swim bladder. In times of real hunger, this scrawny little fish was eaten by early Hawaiians, but more often, due to its oily body, it was dried and burned for fuel in the cooking of other, more savory fishes. To 5".

52

PUFFERS, BOXFISHES, COWFISHES

When threatened by a predator, a puffer fish sucks in a bellyfull of water and almost instantly becomes three times larger. The hungry predator, realizing that the fat little puffer is now too big to fit in his mouth, looks elsewhere for a meal. When removed from the water by curious humans, puffers use the same defense, gulping air instead of water and producing angry grunting noises. As a result, they frequently become lampshades or mantelpieces in the homes of marine collectors. Hawaiians call the puffer 'o'opu hue ("Stomach like a gourd"). It is also sometimes called *make make,* or "deadly death" in corrupted Hawaiian, due to the fact that the organs and sometimes the flesh of certain puffers contain a deadly poison, tetrodotoxin. Although it has wide medical application, the poison can kill quickly if eaten and instances of puffer food poisoning are fatal in 60% of the cases. Even so, puffers are eaten with great relish in Japan, in a dish called *fugu*. Fortunately the dish is prepared very carefully by certified *fugu* cooks, and fatalities are rare.

☐ The sharp-nosed puffers of the Canthigasteridae family are common in Hawaii, and may be distinguished by their long, pointed snouts. Most of them are dainty little fish, rarely exceeding 5" in length. The common puffers, Tetraodontidae family, differ from the sharp-nosed puffers in having short, rounded snouts and more rounded, uniform bodies. The common puffers also grow to be considerably larger than sharp-nosed puffers. The green puffer shown here reaches 10", and some common puffers attain 2 ft. lengths.

☐ The spiny puffers of the Diodontidae family are also adept at puffing themselves up when disturbed. They reach lengths of 2 feet, and it is a strange sight to see a puffed-up, spine-covered basketball with eyes and fins, paddling furiously about the reef. All puffers are carnivores, and possess strong, sharp beaks with which they crush crustaceans, molluscs, echinoderms, and even coral polyps. Careless fishermen are occasionally badly bitten when handling the apparently helpless puffer.

Barred spiny puffer ('o'opu kawa) *Diodon holacanthus* This prickly puffer may be distinguished from the spotted spiny puffer by the large black bars or blotches on its back. This illustration shows a typical spiny puffer in a relaxed cruising mode, with his spines tucked away. Puffers are able to move quite speedily in this configuration. To 10".

Spotted spiny puffer ('o'opu kawa) *Diodon hystrix* Here is a typical puffer doing his balloon number. Note that this fish has small black spots on its back, rather than bars. This poor puffer is very common in Hawaii, grows quite large, and as a consequence is frequently dried and hung to decorate seafood restaurants, or taken home by tourists as a prickly, curious souvenir. To 24".

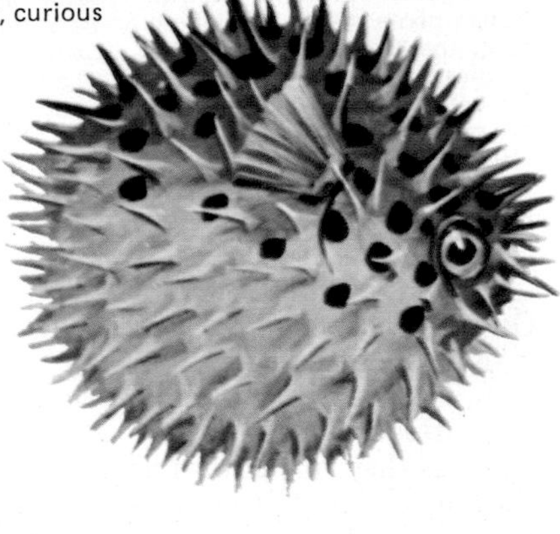

Black-saddled puffer (pu'u olai) *Canthigaster coronata* The Hawaiian name means "lava flow from the hills," and when the saddles on the back of this puffer are distinct, they resemble the lava scars on the slopes of Hawaii. The emaciated appearance and long snout of this fish are distinctive. To 5".

White-spotted puffer *Canthigaster jactator* A beautiful little puffer, one of the most abundant of the family in Hawaii. The large white spots on a dark body serve for identification. One of the smallest of Hawaiian puffers, it grows to 3".

☐ The trunkfishes include the boxfish and cowfish of the Ostraciontidae family. These odd, fascinating little animals are enclosed in a solid, bony box, with holes for the eyes, mouth, fins and vent. Their movements on the reef are curious, almost like miniature helicopters or hovercraft, as they maneuver their rigid, boxed-in bodies with the aid of tiny, fluttering pectoral fins and tail. They are such slow swimmers that they can easily be approached and studied by divers.

Spotted green puffer, striped belly puffer ('opu hue, keke, make make) *Arothron hispidus* Reputed by some Hawaiians to be the most poisonous of all the puffers (*make make* in corrupted Hawaiian means "deadly death"). Some old warriors state that war arrows were dipped in the entrails of this puffer to assure a kill. This has not been verified, but the green puffer is not recommended for the table. Quite common in Hawaii. To 10".

Blue boxfish, spotted trunkfish (moa, mamoa wa'a, o'opa kaku) *Ostracion meleagris* In contrast to the brilliant and gaudy male fish shown here, females of this species are dark blue with white spots. One of their defenses seems to be their ability to exude a poisonous toxin when excited, thus driving off predators. To 6".

Blue-spotted cowfish (maku-kana) *Lactoria fornasini* A fascinating fish to watch, very slow-moving and easy to follow underwater. It is called cowfish because of the horns, the large, expressive eyes, and the bovine expression on the boxed-in face. Quite common in Hawaii. To 6".

56

TUBEMOUTHED FISHES

If you should glance back while skin-diving and see a two-foot length of yellow garden hose peering over your shoulder, don't panic. It's merely one of the curious and quite friendly trumpetfish, or *nu nu*, that seem to be everywhere off Hawaiian reefs. They are astonishing fish to see, as they stare right back at you with their large, independently moveable eyes set at the front of slender, luminous, tubelike bodies. Trumpetfish are specialists at following larger

Oceanic seahorse
Hippocampus kuda To 4''.

Blue-striped pipefish
Doryrhamphus excisus
To 4''.

Shrimpfish, razorfish
Centriscus strigatus
To 4''.

Cornetfish
Fistularia petimba
To 4 feet.

fishes (and even divers) about the reef and sucking in curious smaller fishes in one quick intake of their vacuumlike snouts. A trumpetfish has been seen to insert its snout into a coral crevice and suck a damselfish out of its haven.

The tube-mouthed fishes (order Solenichthys) consist of two sub-orders: one includes the seahorses and pipefishes; the other contains the trumpet, cornet and shrimpfishes. They are all known for their odd, un-fish-like appearance and feeding habits. The tubelike snout is one characteristic they have in common. They are all masters at vacuuming up their food by rapid intakes of water. Most of them possess a partial or complete armor of bony plates, and most of them demonstrate curious spawning behavior where the female deposits her eggs in a brood pouch on the abdomen of the male fish. The eggs are then fertilized by the father and incubated in his brood pouch, and he ejects them live into the sea some 8 to 10 days later. Tube-mouthed fishes range in size from tiny adult pipefishes of 1" to huge adult cornetfish reaching 6 foot lengths. Cornetfish are quite similar to trumpetfish except for the white and green-spotted coloration, and the long filament extending from the tail. Although quite different in appearance, seahorses and pipefishes are very closely related—so closely, in fact, that seahorses are actually pipefishes with a curled-up tail and horse-like tilted heads. They are one or two steps up on the evolutionary scale, according to one theory. Shrimpfish have a compressed, knife-like body, and get their name from their covering of transparent shell-like, shrimp-like armor.

Trumpetfish (nu nu)
Aulostomus chinensis
(yellow coloration) To 24".

Trumpetfish (nu nu)
Aulostomus chinensis
(grey coloration) To 24".

58

MORAY EELS, PUHI

On a population basis, the eels of the order Apodes are very numerous in the reefs throughout the Indo-Pacific. Owing to their secretive nature, however, and their predilection for concealment in reef caves and crevices, their great abundance is not evident to the casual observer. In Hawaii, the largest and most conspicuous family of eels is the Muraenidae, or moray. Though the moray, or *puhi*, can be dangerous, growing to 6 feet of fighting sinew and power, no deaths have been attributed to moray eels. The moray can and will bite with vicious fang-like teeth. Since it can remain well-anchored to its reef hole with its powerful tail, it is a very formidable fighter. Morays are not particularly aggressive toward larger animals, even with all their power. Most of the recorded instances where morays have attacked humans occurred when the moray was caught by a fisherman, or when a diver put a hand into its cave. The display illustrated below, where the moray's head is poised aggressively out of its burrow with fangs bared, is simply the typical curious moray

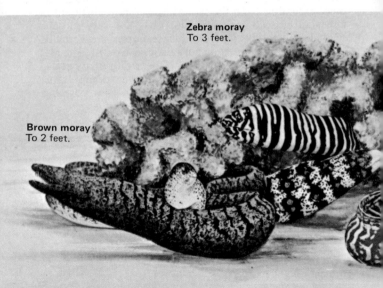

Zebra moray
To 3 feet.

Brown moray
To 2 feet.

Black-speckled moray
To 2 feet.

Snowflake moray
To 2 feet.

surveying his territory. Although the moray opens and closes its mouth constantly, making it appear vicious and aggressive, these mouth movements are the moray's way of breathing by pumping water across its gills. It feeds almost exclusively on small fishes, octopus and crustaceans. The moray has an acute sense of smell, and will forage across the reef at night hunting for small, wounded or sleeping fish. A current theory holds that certain wrasses and parrotfish wrap themselves in a mucous cocoon before sleeping at night as a protection against marauding morays.

Shown below in a typical coral reef habitat are six of the more common Hawaiian *puhi*. The brown moray at the far left, *Gymnothorax eurostus*, is one of the most numerous *puhis* in Hawaii, found along rocky shores at depths of 5 to 50 feet. Perched on the back of the brown moray is the black-speckled moray, *Gymnothorax pictus*, distinctive for its fine black spots on a white body. The two morays at center are both of the *Echidna* genus. The top eel is the brilliantly-colored zebra moray, *Echidna zebra*, with white stripes on a rich ochre body. Just below the

Dragon moray
To 3 feet.

zebra is the snowflake moray, *Echidna nebulosa*, distinctive for the light snowflakes in the center of its dark body bands. The *puhi laumilo*, or undulate moray, *Gymnothorax undulatus*, is shown at the lower right. It has a reputation for viciousness, in spite of its short jaws and small teeth. One of the most ferocious of Hawaiian eels is the dragon moray, *puhi oa* or *puhi kauhila*, *Muraena pardalis*, shown at the far right, top. It is brilliantly colored, with white spots on a rust-orange body. It has been seen to snap at anything going by its burrow.

Undulate moray
To 3 feet.

PART 2
THE OFFSHORE GAME FISHES
AND SHORE GAME AND FOOD FISHES

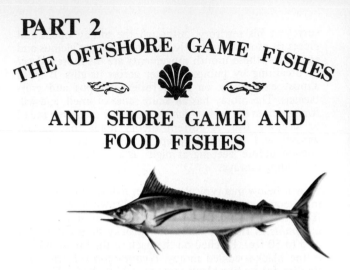

Pacific blue marlin, black marlin, kurokajiki (a'u)
Makaira nigricans To 2000 lbs. Average: 300-400 lbs.

MARLINS, SAILFISHES, SWORDFISHES AND DOLPHINS

The majestic billfishes are the most sought after of all the big game fishes—the true, fighting aristocrats of the sea. In Hawaii, the sport has gained such prominence that annual billfishing tournaments have been established that bring sport fisherman from all over the world. The principal targets of all this activity are the representatives of two fish families: the Istiophoridae, comprising the marlins and sailfishes, or *a'us*, and the Xiphiidae, or swordfishes. Billfishes all possess a sword or bill—a bony projection from the upper jaw—that is apparently used in subduing smaller fishes. They use the sword as a club to maim their victims as they rush through a school of mackerel or similar smaller fishes. A marlin was seen off Kona with a *mahi mahi* impaled on its bill. Hawaii's special attraction for big game fishermen is the abundance of the splendid Pacific blue marlin. The big blue is frequently taken off the Kona Coast, the Penguin Banks and the Waianae Coast by surface trolling as well as by long line fishing.

61

It attains a weight of 2000 lbs. and a length of 11 feet, although the average taken is between 300 and 400 lbs. The world record of the Pacific blue marlin was taken in Hawaiian waters in 1972 for a 1805 lb. fish on a rod and reel. The striped marlin reaches a weight of over 480 lbs.

Striped marlin, kajiki (a'u)
Tetrapturus audax To 480 lbs. Average: 200 lbs.

The striped marlin is known for making spectacular, twisting leaps out of the water. All marlins are impressive fighters, noteworthy for their individuality in fighting compared to other game fish. Some marlins will fight the hook on the surface, twisting and tail-walking, while others will sound deep, which means a long, tedious battle. They are sought more for their fighting spirit than their strong and oily flesh. Conservation-minded fishermen are releasing billfishes and other game fishes after boating them to avoid depletion of these valiant fighting animals.

Sailfish (a'u lepe)
Istiophorus platypterus To 275 lbs. Average: 100 lbs.

A much smaller billfish is the Pacific sailfish, a strikingly beautiful animal with a huge, fan-like dorsal fin. It, too, is abundant in Hawaii but is rarely taken by surface fishermen and only occasionally taken by long line fishermen. The broadbill swordfish rivals the shark in both size and strength. It approaches 1000 lbs. in weight and 15 feet in length, although the average taken is about 250 lbs. Occasionally they will attack boats with their swords, and many a vessel has limped into port leaking badly from attacks by wounded swordfish.

□ Dolphins, or *mahi mahi*, of the Coryphaenidae family, are beautiful, active fish that range all warm seas. They are common around Hawaii and their favorite prey seems to be flying

Broadbill swordfish
Xiphias gladius
To 1000 lbs. Average: 250 lbs.

63

fishes. The terrific speed of the *mahi mahi* enables it to flush the flying fishes like quail, catching them as they fall after a fumbling start or a full flight. On the other hand, the *mahi mahi* suffers from attacks by larger fish, and man. It is popular fare in Hawaiian restaurants and markets. It is a gorgeous fish when caught, with iridescent shades of purplish-bluish gold, sea green and emerald. When death occurs, however, it quickly becomes plain grey in color. The name "dolphin" is confusing, since it is applied to this fish and to the porpoise, which is an aquatic mammal. The two totally different animals can be separated by remembering that the *mahi mahi* dolphin is a water-breathing fish, while the porpoise dolphin is an air-breathing cetacean closely related to the whales.

Dolphin, dorado
(mahi mahi)
Coryphaena hippurus
To 70 lbs. Average: 17 lbs.

TUNAS AND MACKERELS

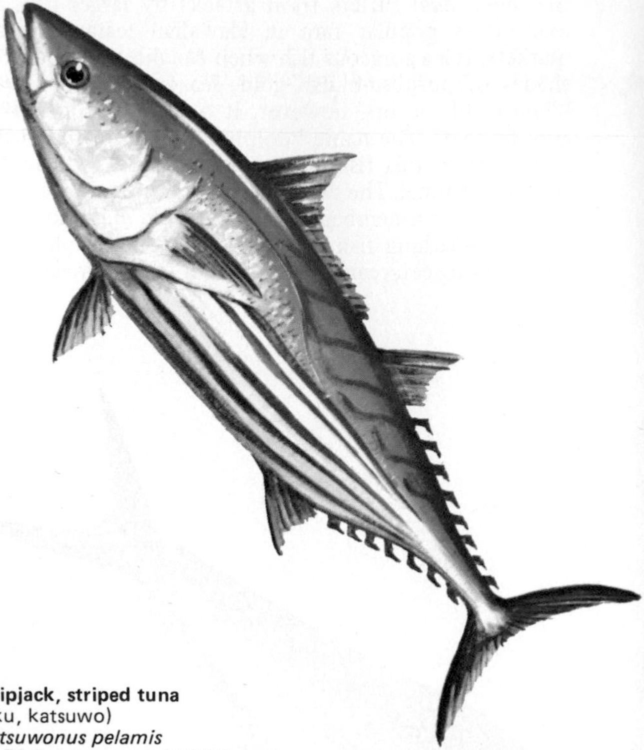

Skipjack, striped tuna
(aku, katsuwo)
Katsuwonus pelamis
To 50 lbs. Average: 10-20 lbs.

The tunas and mackerels of the family Scombridae are high seas fishes of substantial commercial value. In Hawaii, tunas and mackerels make up over 80 percent of the total catch taken by commercial fishermen. The single most important fish is the skipjack tuna, or *aku*, which accounts for well over 50 percent of the annual commercial catch. The yellowfin tuna, or *ahi*, and the marlin are also vital to the fishing fleet catch, but do not compare with the skipjack. Commercial *aku* fishing is a highly specialized business requiring considerable stamina and skill.

The *aku* boat captains search constantly for the flocks of screaming, diving sea birds which feed upon the small fish and squid driven to the surface by the pursuing *aku*. When a school is sighted, the captain runs the boat across the head of the school, slows to a few knots, and live *nehu* and *iao* tuna bait fish are thrown overboard to keep the *aku* circling. The crew moves swiftly to the bamboo poles baited with a feather lure and barbless hook, take their places in the stern, and the action begins. Within a period of 2 hours these experienced fishermen can pump 10 tons of fish aboard.

Yellowfin tuna ('ahi, shibi)
Thunnus albacares
To 300 lbs. Average: 40-50 lbs.

☐ All of the tunas and most of the mackerels are favorite game fish because they are very fast swimmers that strike hard and pull hard, preferring to run and sound down deep, rather than twist and battle the hook. Once a school has been sighted the smart skipper stays near them so as to troll the bait over the noses of the tuna. The thrill of tuna fishing is the long drawn-out battle of sheer weight. Frequently, the fisherman never sees the fish until it is hauled up, completely exhausted, alongside the boat. The skipjack, or *aku*, reaches lengths of 40" and 50 lbs. in weight, although the average caught is 10 to 20 lbs. Another favorite with big game fishermen is the yellowfin tuna, or *'ahi*, a very common tuna in Hawaii. Early Hawaiians named the fish *'ahi*, or "fire," because when a yellowfin took the hook and sounded, the handline went over the side of the outrigger canoe so fast that the line smoked and burned a groove into the side of the canoe. The wahoo, or *ono*, is a long, slender mackerel also known for its fighting prowess. The fish is famed in Hawaii for its excellent flavor; the word *ono* means "sweet." Another small but popular species is the albacore, or *ahipalaha*. It has a well-earned reputation as a fighter and deep-sounder, and provides the finest quality tuna meat of the family. The well-known bonito, or *kawakawa*, is most numerous in Hawaii during the summer months. They are splendid fighters for their size, reaching lengths of 30". The big bluefin tuna, or *maguro*, is the largest of the tunas, attaining a weight of over 800 lbs. They are quite rare in Hawaii, and are occasionally landed by longline fishermen. Needless to say, when a big game fisherman hooks into a mature bluefin, he is in for a long, long battle . . . if he doesn't lose his line.

Bonito, little tuna (kawakawa)
Euthynnus yaito To 20 lbs.
Average: 8-12 lbs.

Bluefin tuna, black tuna (maguro)
Thunnus thynnus To 800 lbs.
Average: 45-80 lbs.

Wahoo (ono)
Acanthocybium solandri
To 120 lbs. Average: 30 lbs.

Albacore (ahipalaha)
Thunnus alalunga
To 90 lbs. Average: 45-80 lbs.

JACKS, CREVALLYS, ULUA

Threadfin (kihikihi ulua)
Alectis ciliaris To 15".

Threadfin (kagami ulua)
Alectis indica To 2 ft.

The *ulua* or jack fishes of the Carangidae family are among the fastest, most voracious fishes of the sea. They are deepwater fishes that range the ocean in schools. Frequently they will sweep in over the reefs to feed on resident fishes. Jacks depend on their speed of attack to kill, and their appetite is prodigious. Their speed and tenacity provide a real challenge to the fisherman who hooks into an *ulua*. It is the toughest fighting fish for its size known. The jack will rarely break out of the water, but takes punishing runs and dives for deep water, and never gives in until it is completely exhausted. It is second only to the bonefish in taking wild, frantic dashes for freedom. Even small juvenile 4" to 8" *uluas*, collectively called *papio* by Hawaiians, are fearless fighters. As a group, the jacks are splendid food fishes, and some of them bring premium prices in the marketplace.

Blue crevally (omilu, hoshi ulua)
Caranx melampygus To 3 ft.

☐ Many of the 200 or so species of jacks are shaped like the *omilu*, or blue crevally, a beautiful fish with scattered blue-black spots or "stars" on its silvery blue-green body. Common in Hawaii, it is one of the jacks most frequently caught by local fishermen. The *pa'u'u* is another very common *ulua*. Both adult and juvenile *pa'u'u* are regularly taken by hook and line fishermen close to shore.

Pa'u'u
Caranx ignobilis
To 3 ft.

□ The colorful amberjack or *kahala* is a fighting jack that dwells well offshore in fairly deep water. It sounds with speed and power, and is a popular game fish that grows to considerable size. A record 120 lb., 8 oz. amberjack was boated off Kona in 1955. The yellow-barred jack or *pa'opa'o ulua* is easily identified by its yellow color and the 8 to 12 dark bands that ring its body. Very young *pa'opa'o* are a brilliant metallic gold in color. The rainbow runner or *kamanu* is a rare but respected game fish that roams the open water. It is a solitary fish, swift and restless, that puts up a ferocious fight when hooked. As it dies, its brilliant rainbow colors fade to dull grey, as does the *mahi mahi*. The most exotic members of the Carangidae family are the fascinating threadfin *uluas,* or *kihikihi uluas.* The two threadfin species common in Hawaiian bays and shallows are alike in the long, trailing threads that stream from their dorsal and anal fins, but *Alectis ciliaris* and *Alectis indica*, as shown, are quite distinct in shape and especially in eye position and head configuration. *A. ciliaris* grows to about 15", while *A. indica* reaches 2 feet on Hawaiian reefs, and is reported to attain 5 feet in Indian waters.

Amberjack, yellowtail
(kahala) *Seriola dumerilii*
To 4 ft.

Rainbow runner (kamanu)
Elagatis bipinnulatus To 3 ft.

Yellow-barred jack
(yellow ulua, pa'opa'o)
Gnathodon speciosus To 3 ft.

MULLETS, BARRACUDA, HERRINGS, AND OTHER FISHES

Fishes, almost every species known on and beyond the reefs, were the prime protein-giving elements of the Hawaiian diet. Daily life in early Hawaii was bound up in the routines of fishing and caring for the fish ponds and plantations. On these two pages I have collected some of the common mullets, herrings and other fishes that were vital as food, bait fish or game fish to the early Hawaiians, and are still avidly sought by shore, net and spear fishermen of today.

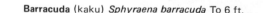

Barracuda (kaku) *Sphyraena barracuda* To 6 ft.

☐ The barracuda grows to 6 feet and is favored by game fishermen as a ferocious fighter. Its nasty reputation as "the tiger of the sea" is probably exaggerated since, at least in Hawaii, it is evasive and has never been known to attack humans. The grey mullet, *'ama'ama*, and the *moi*, or threadfin, are characteristic and much sought-after fishes of the sandy shores, as are the bonefish, ladyfish and milkfish of the herring-like families. In early Hawaii these excellent food fishes were bred and closely guarded in fish ponds to assure their availability for the pot. Today sport fishermen and shore fishermen avidly pursue the wily bonefish, one of the most valiant and hard-running of the shore game fishes, along with the mullet and threadfin. The *nehu*, or anchovy, is the most important tuna bait fish in the islands, and the *'iao*, or silversides, is a common bait fish. The flying fish is a welcome companion on the boat excursions that ply island waters, and was also sought by early Hawaiians as a savory food fish.

Bonefish (o'io) *Albula glossodonta*
To 3 ft.

Grey mullet, striped mullet ('ama'ama) *Mugil cephalus* To 18".

Anchovy (nehu) *Stolephorus purpureus* To 4".

Silversides ('iao) *Pranesus insularum* To 4".

Milkfish (awa) *Chanos chanos* To 3 ft.

Ladyfish (awa'aua) *Elops hawaiiensis* To 2 ft.

Flying fish (malolo) *Cypselurus simas* To 14".

Threadfin (moi) *Polydactylus sexfilis* To 18".

BASSES, GROUPERS, SNAPPERS, AND EMPERORS

**Giant sea bass,
black grouper,
brown grouper**
Promicrops lanceolatus
To 8 ft.

There is no sizeable representation of basses and groupers (family Serranidae) in Hawaii. Further, the identification and classification of the few species is at best dubious. This is due in part to the fact that many basses and groupers, like their cousins, the wrasses, are highly changeable in sex and coloration. All groupers mature first as females and produce eggs. Later in life they reverse sex to become functioning males, which then fertilize the young females. Juveniles are usually quite distinct in color from adults, and many adults are adept at changing their colors and patterns from stripes or bars to blotches and spots to match their background. The giant sea bass attains lengths of up to 8 feet, and is occasionally found in the market-place. During the past two decades only a few sightings and catches of this giant bass have been reported in Hawaii. Scuba divers report rare sightings and catches in or near large sea caves at depths of from 40 to 200 feet. One record 800 lb. sea bass was taken by handline in the harbor at Nawiliwili, Kauai. Another 354 lb. bass was taken by a spear fisherman in 110 feet of water off Lahaina, Maui. The very striking blue-spotted argus, widespread throughout the Indo-Pacific, was recorded from Hawaii over 100 years ago, but was not seen again until it was re-introduced from Moorea, Tahiti, in 1956.

☐ The snappers, of the Lutjanidae family, are excellent food and market fishes, but like the basses, they are not well-represented in Hawaii. Most of the snappers taken here are caught by hook and line over the offshore banks. The grey snapper, or *uku*, is a popular food and sport fish taken regularly off the islands by boat, spear, and shore fishermen. Such red snappers as the *onaga* and the *'ula'ula* are excellent food fishes, quite important commercially in Hawaii, and frequently seen in the Honolulu market. The black-tailed snapper is an attractive inshore fish that was introduced to Hawaii from Moorea, Tahiti, in 1956 in hopes it would thrive here. The bigeye emperor, or *mu*, is apparently the only representative of the Sparidae family in Hawaiian waters. An excellent food fish, it was once plentiful in Hawaiian markets, but is now quite rare, and commands a high price when available.

Blue-spotted argus, black grouper
Cephalopholis argus To 18".

Black-tailed snapper
Lutjanus fulvus To 18".

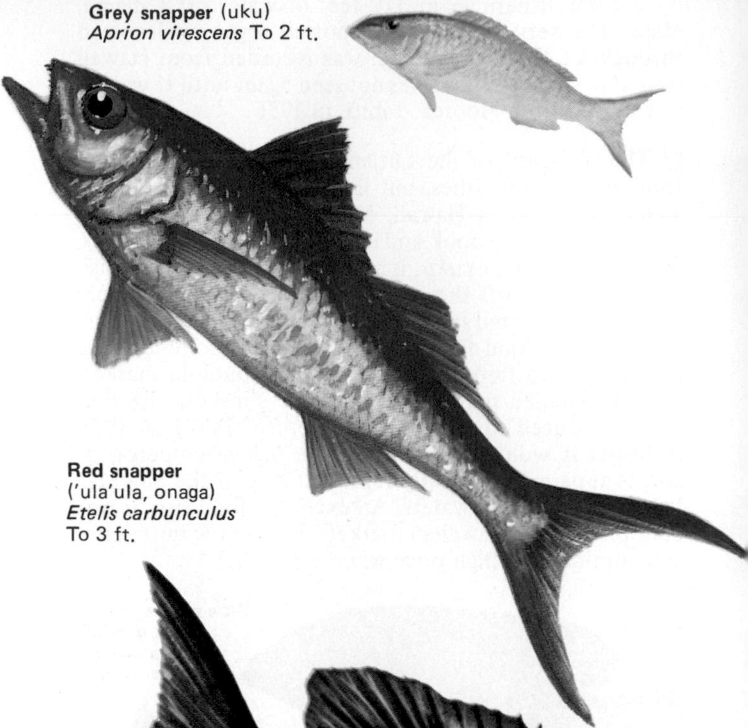

Grey snapper (uku)
Aprion virescens To 2 ft.

Red snapper
('ula'ula, onaga)
Etelis carbunculus
To 3 ft.

Bigeye emperor
(mu, mamamu, medai)
Monotaxis grandoculis
To 22".

SHARKS AND RAYS

For the interested swimmer who considers skin or scuba diving as a sport, probably one of the greatest fears is the shark attack. Popular misconceptions engendered by movies, TV, books and newspaper stories contribute to the image of this brute of the sea as being literally waiting offshore to pounce on anyone who ventures into the water, especially in tropical seas. Yet actual shark sightings around shallow reefs are rare, and incidents of attacks on humans off most of the world's beaches and reefs are extremely rare. In Hawaii, for example, in the past 85 years since records have been kept, only 16 people have been attacked by sharks, and only five of these attacks were fatal. Considering the multitude of tourists, surfers, divers and fishermen who swarm daily about Hawaiian shores, this number is remarkably small. One authority states that the probability of shark attack in Hawaii is about the same as that of being struck by lightning. The safety of Hawaiian waters is due in part to regular sharkfishing programs carried out over the past decades to reduce the numbers of sharks. Most sharks are not reef-dwelling fishes, but they make occasional visits to the reefs to feed on resident fishes and detritus. Divers who spear or maim fish may attract sharks to their area by the low frequency vibrations and scent trails that emanate from the wounded fish.

Great white shark (niuhi)
Carcharodon carcharius To 35 ft.

Hammerhead shark (mano kihikihi) *Sphyrna lewini* To 12 ft.

Great blue shark (mano) *Prionace glauca* To 12 ft.

White-tipped reef shark (lalakea) *Triaenodon obesus* To 10 ft.

Tiger shark (mano, niuhi) *Galeocerdo cuvier* To 30 ft.

Sandbar shark, brown shark *Carcharhinus plumbeus* To 10 ft.

□ Sharks and rays of the Elasmobranchii group of fishes are distinct from all of the foregoing bony fishes because their skeletons are composed of cartilage instead of bone. Of some 250 shark species inhabiting the seas of the world, about 15 species have been recorded from Hawaii. The tiger shark is easily identified by the indistinct vertical bars and spots along its sides. It is probably the dreaded *niuhi* of Hawaiian legend. Polynesians and Hawaiians endowed most sharks, especially the large maneaters, with supernatural powers. Due to their dependence on and familiarity with the sea, they were well aware of the awful power of the large, hungry shark, and so they came to see the shark as a god in disguise. Rituals were carefully evolved and scrupulously observed to bring the blessings of the shark-god. The great white shark is occasionally taken in deep offshore waters, as is the great blue shark. Small white-tipped sharks and sandbar sharks are occasionally seen in certain reef areas, especially such low, leeward reefs as French Frigate Shoals, Laysan and Lisianski Island. Two types of hammerhead sharks are represented in Hawaiian waters, but the scalloped hammerhead shown is by far the more numerous.

Stingrays and pig-faced rays of the Batoidei order are common around Hawaii. The spotted eagle ray, or *hihimanu*, is one of the most striking and attractive of the family. They are commonly seen singly or in small schools, winging gracefully between coral heads, or hovering almost motionless just beyond the breaker line. The brown stingray is more often seen resting or half-submerged in reef bottom sand. All of our rays are quite harmless if left alone, but they possess nasty, sometimes poisonous spines on their whiplike tails, and they should be admired at a safe distance. Manta rays, or "devil" rays, of the Mobulidae family are common about the outer reefs, and have often been photographed by local scuba divers. In spite of the name "devil" ray, mantas are now recognized to be large, docile creatures, reaching 12 feet from wingtip to wingtip, that cruise channel areas and outer reefs feeding on small crustaceans and other planktonic food.

Eagle ray (hihimanu)
Aetobatus narinari To 4 ft.

Brown stingray
Dasyatis hawaiiensis To 4 ft.

Manta ray, devil ray
Manta alfredi To 12 ft.

DIVING TIPS AND REEF MAP GUIDES
TO THE HAWAIIAN ISLANDS
(See following four pages)

The Hawaiian Islands are a fish-watcher's paradise for the interested swimmer-tourist. Whether you are on Oahu or Hawaii, Maui or Kauai, Lanai or Molokai, the underwater world of the reefs is only minutes away. All that is needed is the ability to swim, and the effort required to adjust to swimming with a face mask and snorkel tube. These can be purchased at most sporting goods stores for under $25.00. Swim fins are advised for strong swimmers capable of long skin-diving excursions. The fins give you the added push necessary for effortless cruising around the reefs. The warmth of the water (75° to 80°F) allows for comfortable swimming in your bathing suit. No wet suit is needed.

To aid the diver in locating Hawaii's coral reef fishes, I have provided maps on the following four pages that locate Hawaii's splendid beaches, bays and parks, and that indicate the heavier concentrations of coral reefs on the six larger islands. Also shown are preferred and proven game fishing areas, shore fishing zones and diving areas that are well-explored and well-populated with fishes. A rental car obtainable through your hotel will take you along excellent highways to any beach, park or coral reef of your choice.

The coral reef areas of Waikiki Beach (see map of Oahu) are excellent for skin and SCUBA diving, as is Maunalua Bay, Waimanolo Beach, Kaneohe Bay, Punaluu Beach and Kawela Bay. Hanauma Bay, near Koko Head, is highly recommended for beginning divers and experienced aquanauts. Hawaii has declared this coral reef bay an underwater park, where no spear fishing or taking of reef animals is allowed, and the fishes seem to know it. They swarm around the coral reefs there, and a half hour of slow reef cruising will reveal many, if not all, of the reef fishes shown in this book.

A few words of caution are called for, however, before you plunge into the surf. Skindiving is easy and pleasurable when practiced in calm, clear-water bays and beaches. Exercise normal caution when swimming among close-packed coral reefs. If you aren't careful, wave action can pitch you unexpectedly into coral heads that may inflict painful scratches and wounds that are difficult to heal. Watch where you are in relation to the shore and nearby reefs at all times, and make allowances for wave action. Avoid overtiring yourself, and always swim accompanied by a companion. Be sure to keep hands and feet out of reef holes and crevices, and avoid areas of high surf, turbulence and choppy water. SCUBA (self-contained underwater breathing apparatus) diving will provide even greater and deeper access to Hawaii's underwater world, but the beginner requires detailed instruction and certification by a skilled diver before crossing this frontier. Qualified SCUBA instructors abound on most of Hawaii's islands. Consult the phone book or your hotel registrar for information.

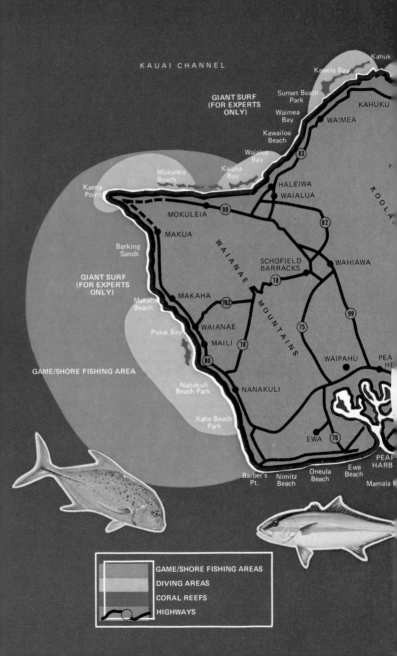

KAUAI CHANNEL

Kahuk
Kawela Bay

GIANT SURF
(FOR EXPERTS
ONLY)

Sunset Beach
Park

Waimea
Bay

KAHUKU

WAIMEA

Kawailoa
Beach

(83)

KOOLA

Waialua
Bay

Mokuleia
Beach

Kaiaka
Bay

HALEIWA

Kaena
Point

WAIALUA

MOKULEIA   (99)

(82)

MAKUA

Barking
Sands

WAIANAE

SCHOFIELD
BARRACKS

WAHIAWA

GIANT SURF
(FOR EXPERTS
ONLY)

Makaha
Beach

MAKAHA

(782)

(78)

MOUNTAINS

(99)

(75)

Pokai Bay

WAIANAE

MAILI   (78)

WAIPAHU

PEA
HE

(90)

GAME/SHORE FISHING AREA

Nanakuli
Beach Park

NANAKULI

Kahe Beach
Park

EWA   (76)

PEAR
HARB

Barber's
Pt.

Nimitz
Beach

Oneula
Beach

Ewa
Beach

Mamala

GAME/SHORE FISHING AREAS

DIVING AREAS

CORAL REEFS

HIGHWAYS

OAHU

Makahoa Pt.
HUKILAU AREA
Laie Bay

POLYNESIAN
CULTURAL CENTER

Kaipapau Pt.

Punaluu Beach
Park

Kahana Bay

GOOD SWIMMING,
EASY SURFING

Kaawa Beach Park

KAAWA

Mokolii Island

KANEOHE
BAY

Kapapa Island

Moku Manu

Coral
Garden

MOKAPU PENINSULA

KAHALUU

(83)

Kailua Bay

KANEOHE

KAILUA

Mokulua Islands

LANIKAI

AIEA

Waimanolo Bay

(63) (61)

WAIMANOLO

Rabbit Island

Keehi
Lagoon

HONOLULU

Makapuu Pt.

SEA LIFE
PARK

(72)

Ala Moana
Park

Blow Hole

WAIKIKI BEACH

Kahala Beach

Hanauma Bay

DIAMOND
HEAD

Maunalua Bay

KOKO HEAD

HANAUMA BAY
UNDERWATER
CORAL REEF PARK

EXCELLENT SWIMMING,
DIVING, PICNIC AREA

KAIWI CHANNEL

TAINS

WATER SKIING AREA

KAUAI

HAENA Hanalei Bay KILAUEA
Lumahai Beach   Kilauea Bay

Bird of Paradise
Beach   Anahola Bay

Barking Sands   ANAHOLA

Kokee Park

WAILUA

LIHUE   Hanamaulu Bay

LAWAI   Nawiliwili
               Harbor
Waimea Bay

Hanapepe   Poipu Beach Park
Bay   Prince Kuhio
         Park

NIIHAU

OAHU

SEE
PRECEDING
PAGES

Kalaup

Kaena Pt.

Lanai City
Kaumalapa

LANA

K

GAME/SHORE FISHING AREAS
DIVING AREAS
CORAL REEFS
HIGHWAYS

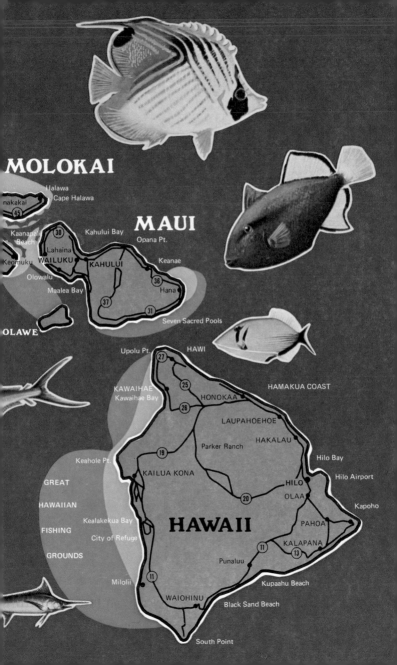

MOLOKAI

Halawa
Cape Halawa
nakakai
45

MAUI

Kaanapali Beach
30
Kahului Bay
Opana Pt.
Lahaina
WAILUKU
KAHULUI
Keanae
Keomuku
Olowalu
36
Maalea Bay
37
Hana
31
Seven Sacred Pools

OLAWE

Upolu Pt.
HAWI
27
KAWAIHAE
Kawaihae Bay
25
HAMAKUA COAST
26
HONOKAA
LAUPAHOEHOE
HAKALAU
19
Parker Ranch
Keahole Pt.
Hilo Bay
KAILUA KONA
HILO
Hilo Airport
20
OLAA
GREAT
Kapoho
HAWAIIAN
Kealakekua Bay
PAHOA
FISHING
City of Refuge
HAWAII
KALAPANA
11
GROUNDS
13
Punaluu
Milolii
11
Kupaahu Beach
WAIOHINU
Black Sand Beach
South Point

BIBLIOGRAPHY

I would like to express my appreciation to the authors of the following works and others too numerous to mention here. New publications, like living coral reefs, are not possible without building on the creations of earlier workers. Publications best suited to the general reader are starred with an asterisk.

*Gosline, W. A. and Brock, V. E. (1960). *Handbook of Hawaiian Fishes.* Honolulu: University of Hawaii Press.

Jordan, D. S. and Evermann, B. W. (1905). *The Shore Fishes of the Hawaiian Islands.* Bulletin of the U.S. Fish Commission.

Fowler, H. W. (1928-1949). *The Fishes of Oceania.* Vol. 10 plus 3 supplements. Honolulu: Bishop Museum.

Smith, J.L.B. (1958). *The Sea Fishes of Southern Africa.* Johannesburg: Trustees of the Sea Fishes of Southern Africa Book Fund.

Schultz, L. P., et al. (1953-1960). *Fishes of the Marshall and Marianas Islands.* Washington, D.C.: U.S. Nat. Museum Bulletin.

*Hobson, E. S. and Chave, E. H. (1972). *Hawaiian Reef Animals.* Honolulu: University of Hawaii Press.

*Tinker, S. W. (1978). *Fishes of Hawaii: A Handbook of the Marine Fishes of Hawaii and the Central Pacific Ocean.* Honolulu: Hawaiian Service, Inc.

*Randall, J. E. (1980). *The Underwater Guide to Hawaiian Reef Fishes.* Newtown Square, Pa.: Harrowood Books.

Axelrod, H. R. and Emmens, C.W. (1969). *Exotic Marine Fishes.* Jersey City, N. J.: TFH Publications.

*Herald, E. S. (1961). *Living Fishes of the World.* New York: Doubleday and Company, Inc.

La Gorce, J. O. (1961). *The Book of Fishes.* Washington, D.C.: National Geographic Society.

*Titcomb, M. (1972). *Native Use of Fish in Hawaii.* Honolulu: University of Hawaii Press.

*MacKellar, J. S. (1968). *Hawaii Goes Fishing.* Tokyo: Charles E. Tuttle Co., Inc.

Hosaka, E. Y. (1944). *Sport Fishing in Hawaii.* Honolulu: Bond's.

*Yasuda, F. and Hiyama, Y., et al. (1972). *Pacific Marine Fishes.* Hong Kong: TFH Publications, Inc. Ltd.

*Bridges, W. (1970). *Book of the Water World.* New York: New York Zoological Society.

*Cust, G. and Cox, G. (1972). *Tropical Aquarium Fishes.* Holland: Hamlyn Publishing Group Ltd.

*Axelrod, H. R. and Voerderwinkler, W. (1967). *Salt Water Aquarium Fish.* Jersey City, N. J.: TFH Publications.

*Cox, G. F. (1972). *Tropical Marine Aquaria.* New York: Grosset and Dunlap, Inc.

*O'Connell, R. F. (1969). *The Marine Aquarium.* St. Petersburg, Florida: Great Outdoors Publishing Company.

*Ravensdale, T. (1971). *Coral Fishes.* St. Petersburg, Florida: Great Outdoors Publishing Company.

INDEX TO FISHES

89